Julia Summerland • Love in Times of Coronavirus

To Katarina and Maurice

"*A compelling tale about looking for love in unsettling times. Julia Summerland's novel gives you the butterflies and leaves you happy and hopeful. Grab a cup of tea, snuggle up, and enjoy the read.*" *(Katarina)*

Julia Summerland

LOVE IN TIMES OF CORONAVIRUS

Edition AVRA

Bibliographic Information of the German National Library
The German National Library has registered this publication
in the German National Bibliography;
detailed bibliographic information can be found online at http://dnb.d-nb.de.
© Edition AVRA: A trademark of Frieling & Huffmann GmbH & Co. KG
Phone: 0 30 / 766 999-0
www.frieling.de
Cover illustration: Emilia Agovic
Image source: pixabay
1st Edition 2020
ISBN (print) 978-3-8280-3566-9
ISBN (e-book) 978-3-8280-3567-6
All rights reserved Printed in Germany

CONTENTS

With the exception of public figures, all the characters depicted in this book are creatures of Julia's imagination and any resemblance to any real person is coincidental.

Julia was so bored during the time of lockdown that she came up with this book, which is all fiction. However, the events around the Covid-19 pandemic in the first half of 2020 were very real and are described as they happened.

During all her encounters, Julia followed social distancing and lockdown rules as they were and are in Luxembourg (except for possibly one kiss...).

In the time of coronavirus, Julia registered on an online dating platform to combat the loneliness she had been experiencing since her long-time boyfriend had left her. In this book, she meets various men. The meetings – sometimes funny, sometimes sad – make up the story. It begins sometime in March 2019 and ends in July 2020.

How will the story continue? Will Julia find love? How will coronavirus continue to spread? Will there be a second, or even a third, lockdown? Will she find love in times of coronavirus? Please read her story!

PRACTICAL ADVICE

FOR THE LOVELORN

Preface by BM

"My dear Julia,

Please regard this search for a relationship as a business process. Imagine you are looking for someone to do business with. You have to go through ten disappointments to get one deal closed. The same way you do not take the failure of a business deal as a personal failure please do not consider all these efforts as personal failures either. The same way you have been 'hit' in your relationship after so many years of investment in it, those males who are contacting you have also gone through a similar process. They are also 'survivors' of great disappointments. Failure in relationships is a result of a combination of states of mind of two people who are scared to death and who are eager to re-establish their self-confidence.

In your coming meetings with your future potential partners, please try to listen for around 75% of the time and talk for about 25% of the time. You will be surprised how well it works. People like to talk about themselves. Try to be positive throughout the conversation. Do not explain and do not complain. Your potential partners will be mesmerized by your positive attitudes and they will become positive too.

Spending 5 hours in a pub with a candidate for future relationships, as you have indicted in your last letter, is a sign of weakness. It reflects badly on you as if you have nothing better to do than sitting in a pub. You should cut short your first five meetings with a 'new' person and leave after a maximum of 75 minutes with a time excuse. Also, all these first meetings should take place in a public place! You must meet in a restaurant, pub, sport club, garden, ski arena, etc. Nobody should come to pick you up from home. Make yourself a little mysterious... create some tension..."

BM

"Strong minds discuss ideas, average minds discuss events, weak minds discuss people."

(Socrates)

My colleague and good friend, Julia, has been looking for relationships. Not that she does not have millions of contacts, acquaintances and good friends, but she wanted to use a platform for online dating to answer the question of how to classify and select close friends based on their written, and, eventually, spoken communication skills.

In no time did Julia realize that the platform alone was not appropriate for such an investigation because, after all, she only sampled the non-female half of the population, and also because the messages she received were mostly composed by desperate males trying to get a free ride, believing they disguised their purpose well enough.

Yet, funnily, these messages seem to plagiarize each other. Hence the idea of compiling all those messages as well as stories about face-to-face encounters and sharing their comic side with the readers. It is neither an act of 'revenge' nor a criticism of the other gender. After all Julia appreciates men as much as she appreciates women. The purpose of this collection is to depict people as they are, for good and for bad, and to continue to love them with their strengths and weaknesses. It is an artistic depiction of a mirror image of ourselves that describes people and events that will allow you to reflect on other people's experience to better understand yourself, the 'games' you play and how these 'games' are perceived and interpreted by others.

The activities described here took place during the coronavirus crisis, a terrible worldwide pandemic that started in Wuhan, China, and from there spread rapidly worldwide, provoking never-before-seen complete lockdowns of cities and countries, shutting national borders, and imprisoning people in their own homes.

This change in lifestyle, including working from home instead of from the office, has had major impacts on our social, economic and moral lives. How to survive in such a challenging environment? How to date online and how to date in general with social distancing measures in place? How to combat loneliness with self-isolation and home confinement? Are dating and love possible in coronavirus times? Is e-mailing the new mode of dating and what would happen to carnal love? How will Julia solve her issue of dating in coronavirus times? Is it possible that a few men will compete to capture Julia's heart? Or some of them will manage to seduce her concurrently? How do you think the story will evolve? Do you have a similar story to tell? Do you have even more fantastic or bizarre experience you are willing to share? Please feel free to anonymously share your story with the author of this book.

Enjoy reading the emails, messages and letters, as well as about the dates and, please, keep smiling. (BM)

Preface by Patricia

Your search for a partner has certainly been very wide-ranging, Julia. However, I wonder, do you still remember the names of the men you met? While hearing your stories, I feel quite dizzy. I suppose some of these men are failures, you simply put them aside and forgot about them. Like the mama's boy – *mammone*, as the Italians say – who still lives with his mother, or the other one who was too stingy to pay for a movie ticket. The others, well, you need to sort them carefully, maybe your prince charming is among them. If not, restart from the beginning. You simply recover like a tumbler and keep going. That's my advice to you.

The first case of coronavirus was detected in Wuhan province in China in December 2019.

WORDS ABOUT BOYFRIENDS

Gregory

Before all this began: a Sunday sometime in March 2019

"I will not leave my wife," said Gregory.

We were on our bikes and this was the first sentence he said to me after leaving from my place in Luxembourg city. It was a cold but sunny day in March. It was not one of my best days. In the morning, I had been teaching a fitness class. Gregory looked at me during the class and said, "What about going for a bike ride this afternoon?"

"With pleasure", I replied, "Where shall we go to?"

"We can do the bicycle path – the *piste cyclable* – I can come to your place and we'll start from there. Two o'clock is good for you?"

"Yes, perfect."

Gregory came by car to my place, with his bike in his car, parked in the courtyard behind my apartment building and we started cycling from there, riding through Merl, Belair, Mamer and heading to Clémency. We cycled behind one another in town but after he rode next to me and said his famous sentence: "I will not leave my wife."

"Well", I thought, "Why is he telling me this? I don't really understand."

We continued cycling, it was turning out to be a pleasant day, finally the first really sunny day for weeks. As usual, Luxembourg is grey, sometimes without any decent sunshine for months in winter. So it was very nice enjoying the sunshine on the bike and the company of Gregory. I asked him so many questions. "Do you have children?" "Did you study?" "Where, what, when?" "What do you do in life? What do you do all day long?"

We arrived at the old Clémency train station, where people were enjoying food and drinks on a terrace in the sun. We sat down at one of the tables, ordered a non-alcoholic beer and Gregory said, "Now, tell me about you, what makes you so sad?"

I started talking about my lost love with Alan. "After so many years together, he has left me, of course, for a younger woman. I am very sad. Not only this but also in my family, we lived through a tragedy. This is the reason why I am so sad. It is not easy for me to hide my feelings, in front of the classes. You noticed that I was sad, others noticed as well. You see, I am an independent teacher and it is not simple, especially for a woman, being independent, and alone. Ironically, Alan left me exactly at the moment I asked him for help. But well, this is how it is, life goes on, it is difficult. But I will not get back together with him. We had a wonderful time, with unforgettable moments and travelling all over the world."

Gregory advised, "You see, nobody can take these wonderful moments from you. Keep them for yourself, in your heart, and treasure them. Also, nobody can take this special moment here from us. We will treasure it."

In the following months, we met from time to time, and later more frequently, to go cycling and do other sporting activities. I remember fondly the ice skating and curling at Kockelscheuer and the time we went rock climbing in Berdorf in July 2019.

Despite the great friendship we felt for each other, Gregory continued to confirm at nearly every encounter that he would never leave his wife. Finally, I told Gregory that I could not continue this kind of relationship, and that I was looking for a serious partner.

"Gregory, I love you so much, I cannot stand the fact that you are living together with your wife in the same house, you cook with her, you eat with her, you share a bed with her. This is impossible for me. You call me when you are free, when your wife lets you go, but not when I need you. Only when you are free do you call me and I should be there for you, because you find you have time from two to three in the afternoon or after a sports lesson, because you tell your wife your shower has taken longer than usual. This is impossible. It is over between us. It is over."

Gregory told me, "If you do this, then you will be all alone!"

What the girlfriends said

In one of my sports classes I told my friend Agnès about my bad luck with men. I told Agnès that Alan had left me for another woman, a younger woman, after so many years of relationship. I told Agnès that Gregory would never leave his wife. Agnès' answer was clear and direct: "Forget about them, both of them. If Alan has left you for another woman, then he is stupid. If Gregory doesn't leave his wife, then you are wasting your time on him. Don't waste your time on him. You should go register on Meetyourlove, the dating agency site, and find for your special someone. You deserve a serious partner. You just need to be patient and search for him on Meetyourlove. You will find him. I know it. My own daughter found her husband on Meetyourlove. They have been married for eight years now and have a baby girl."

Agnès repeated this same message over and over again for many months. She never stopped telling me to register on Meetyourlove and to find the love of my life there. For months, I always replied the same way.

"No."

"I don't want to."

"I am not ready yet."

"I don't believe in it."

"I don't know."

The same day that Gregory told me "then you will be all alone, lonesome on your own", I decided to register on Meetyourlove.

My friend Petra also told me that I should definitely say no to Gregory.

"Do not waste your time on a married man who will never leave his wife. You will find somebody who is free and who sticks with you. So you will not be alone on week-ends, on Christmas day, New Year's Eve, your birthday and you could call him whenever you want, without having to wait until he is free from three to four because his wife went shopping or whatever. You deserve better than this."

Alan

We had a long-lasting relationship of many years, but unfortunately Alan left me for another woman, a younger one of course. The simple fact is, I loved him very much and I still love him, despite the fact that he left me. I also love his two sons. We used to travel the world and the most memorable trips were our bicycling holidays.

THE MEN PRESENT THEMSELVES

Jordan

Jordan called. "How are you, Julia?" he asked, "Are you ok? What are you doing all day long alone at home?"

He continued talking about being alone. In self-isolation, he had the need to talk. I listened.

Jordan told me, "I want you to be part of my family. I will divorce my wife and marry you. I have children and you don't have children. This would be the chance for you to have children, my children would be yours. I love you so much. Kisses. Sleep well, good night my Julia!"

The man from Metz

He was my first ever contact on Meetyourlove but what a disappointment in the end. First impressions? Really sporty, good looking, same age, just a little younger than me, very much into cycling and running like me. Later, it became clear that he thought he was a superhero because of his professional position as a bank director. When he heard about my job, he became a little bit humbler. We exchanged phone numbers and WhatsApp details, he sent photos of himself – very good looking – and wanted to meet me. He sent a very nice music video via WhatsApp starring Pamela Anderson. And then, that was it... I never heard from him again!

Bernard

"My Julia:

Darling, a great idea - just behave like men. Do not take any s*** from any man.

I am delighted to learn that your students deliver. After all, they have a great teacher. It is so good that you are engaged in teaching – it gives you balance in your life."

"Here is an article of how men and women may differ in some aspect of their behaviour....

Good luck :))"

— — — — —

"I am not exactly sure what it means to behave like a man. Do you mean in terms of relationships? I assume it depends on the man. But the reality is that it has been a long time since I was in the dating market and I have no clue about current norms. Also, I never played the female role :)))

Just take a break and re-evaluate your position."

— — — — —

"If you hate the process of dating men why do you go through it so intensively? Why don't you declare a moratorium? Also, why do you still see Alan after your history with him? I am lucky indeed that I do not have to go through these processes.

I am sure you are doing all this to be with Alan again in the end. You still love him, you always loved him. Eventually you will end up with Alan again.

Anyhow, good luck. Don't forget, they are all A.H."

— — — — —

"...Just like dating, it is unpleasant but not life threatening.

Why don't you take a break? What would happen if for a month or two you were not looking for a man?

Peace."

— — — — —

"I recommended to a friend of mine whose wife had left him to log onto a dating website. He got tired very quickly. It is time and energy consuming.

XXX"

— — — — —

"My dear darling Julia:

I knew (and probably you knew too) that Gregory would not leave his wife. So be it. I am sure you will find a nice person who is not married and who will be a good partner, and not one of your students. It does not make any sense to date your students. Your dates should always be people out of town. As you said, you live in a small village and everybody knows everybody else's 'cooking.'

It is rainy but no wind...

Kisses to you my darling,

Bernard

— — — — —

"Strength is in the mind... if you believe you can do something then you will do it. Enjoy your meeting with Oliver. Hope he is not yet another A.H. Let's see if he pays for the meal :)))

XXX

— — — — —

"I am glad your date was nice to you. I hope he is not married - please check it out. I could not open the website for which you sent me the link. I saw his picture on his company's website :)

Raining but not cold. Working as usual."

— — — — —

"Dating.

Much easier to date an unmarried man than a married one. I hope he lives far enough from your place so when you separate you won't have to see him anymore. Hope he is not one of your students.

You are persistent – there is no question about it :)

Anyhow, you will return in the end to Alan.

Xxx"

— — — — —

"Darling,

How good a dancer are you?

I used to dance pretty well...

Memories..."

Joris

The next one was Joris. On Meetyourlove and on the phone, he pretended to be a good cyclist. He talked about himself as if he was a sportsman, just like the one I was looking for!

He said, "I am doing my spinning class now, we could meet after that and have lunch. What do you think, where do you want to meet? Would the park in Hesperange be a place where we could go for a walk?"

"Where exactly do you want to meet?"

"The carpark in the centre of Hesperange."

"Which one? There are a few."

"The one in front of the bank."

It was a Saturday afternoon. As I like being early and observing who arrives, how and under what circumstances, I was early at the carpark and was waiting in my car for him. And then I saw a man coming up to my car. He was limping, he looked old, grey, was dressed all in black, and my first reaction was:

"Oh, no, I do hope that's not him!"

But it definitely was him.

He greeted me by pointing at his head.

"Shall we go for a walk?" he asked. It was cold and rainy and grey.

He said, "We could go through the park, or we could go along the street, ah, let's go along the street. My fingers are cold, it is so cold. My fingers are really frozen, this is too cold for me."

He went for this walk, but then he repeated that his fingers were frozen because it was too cold. He suggested we go for a hot tea in the café at the crossing, which is what we did.

We talked a bit and then he paid for the tea.

"I need to go grocery shopping now, like every Saturday afternoon", he said, "I always go later in the afternoon because there are less people."

Later, we continued writing WhatsApp messages and I suggested in a message, "What about going to see a movie tomorrow? What do you think?"

He wrote back, "I do not think anything." Obviously, this meant he was not interested. Supposedly, the movie tickets were too expensive for him. I never heard from him again.

Thomas

Met on Meetyourlove on a Sunday morning in February 2020, at precisely seven in the morning.

I liked him on the site. He liked me back. He wrote. I answered with my phone number. He called me. "What are you doing at seven o'clock on a Sunday morning on Meetyourlove?" he wanted to know.

"And you?" I asked.

We agreed to meet just after lunch at two at my place in Luxembourg to go for a walk in the city. This was just before the big storm that was forecast for six. Everybody was saying to make sure you are inside before then because a huge storm was expected.

Thomas and I met at his car in front of my apartment. I asked him about his family. He told me about his life, his family and his profession. We started walking to go into town. My phone rang.

"Hello."

"This is Oliver, are you Julia?"

"Yes, please may I call you back later in the afternoon, maybe in the evening?"

"Of course. Talk to you later."

Thomas looked at me and asked, "Who was that?"

I said, "A friend of mine." But this was a lie. It was another man I had seen on Meetyourlove the same morning, and this was the first contact.

Thomas and I continued our walk, I showed him around Luxembourg city, the Adolphe Bridge, the cathedral, the protestant church with its Anglican service, St Michel's church and the Wenzel tourist walk. We took pictures. It was a good afternoon. The storm started; the wind became stronger. We decided to walk back to his car so that he could drive back home before the storm.

The following week, we phoned quite a few times, and we wrote WhatsApp messages.

One evening, Thomas called me, I had the impression he was a bit drunk, or even a lot drunk. Straight off he told me, "I have met a wonderful woman on Meetyourlove. She will be coming to see me tonight". He continued, "I loved our walk in Luxembourg" and added that he would like to invite me to his town for a bike ride and a dinner, and to stay overnight. I never heard from him again. Or at least, I thought I would not, sometimes life turns out differently.

Oliver

Met on Meetyourlove on the same Sunday morning in February 2020, just after Thomas.

And he called while I was walking with Thomas on our tour of the town. We were walking past the Italian Embassy at around two thirty.

He had written on Meetyourlove:

"Moien, Hi Julia, Nice meeting you here. I see you are also living in Lux. We have many things in common ... interesting."

"Hi Oliver, you can call me at 611.111.111. Julia."

"Hallo Julia, nice to hear from you. Thank you for your telephone number. May I call you tomorrow early afternoon, as I will do some sports in the morning? I am looking forward to it. Oliver."

"Dear Oliver, yes, my pleasure, you also can call me now, or in the afternoon, as you wish. I will be certainly be cycling also. Kind regards, Julia."

"Good morning Julia, right now am doing spinning and fitness :-) Until later. Oliver."

So, there we were, Thomas and I, walking past the Italian Embassy in Rue Goethe when Oliver called me.

"Hello Julia, how are you?" he asked.

His voice was very warm. I thought to myself, I like the sound of this voice.

I asked him, "Could I please call you later in the afternoon?"

"Yes, no problem."

After my walk through town with Thomas, I called Oliver. Thomas had barely just left in his car when I called Oliver.

I couldn't know then that this would be one of the longest phone calls in my life. Outside there was the storm, as predicted with strong winds and rain. Oliver and I stayed on the phone for six hours. From four in the afternoon until ten that night. The battery of his phone went flat twice, he had to recharge it twice! That was so funny.

It did not begin well. We had hardly exchanged a few sentences when he told me:

"You are fake!"

Baffled, I replied, "Why should I be fake? I am real!"

"Why do you speak English and German? Why do you know so much?"

"Because it is me! I am real!"

"It's just that some weeks ago somebody had called me pretending she was from Meetyourlove, but she was a fake, a Canadian."

"Oliver, sorry, but I am not fake. How can I show you that I am real?"

"Ok, no, yes, I am sorry, but please try to understand me! And please be extra careful in your future contacts on Meetyourlove, there are many fake people! You need to be very careful please!"

I found him fascinating. We talked and talked. He found me fascinating.

At the beginning, I was sitting at my desk, then I began getting hungry and started eating purée with black olives. I heard him eating as well and asked: "What are you eating?"

"Black olives."

Him too! He sent me the picture of the olives he was eating. He sent me pictures of his last cycling holiday and spoke about having to keep his bike in his hotel room and washing it in the shower. He told me that his next trip would also be a biking one.

He asked, "Do you want to come with me?"

We talked about our lost relationships, about our jobs, our holidays and about our lives.

After a while, I went to bed and continued talking with him until we decided that it was getting a bit late and that on Monday morning we both had to get up early and it would be better to get some sleep, even though we still had so many stories to tell.

He said, "You will tell me all of this when we meet in person."

I really liked him from the start. I found him captivating. We spoke a mix of English and German.

We exchanged WhatsApp details and started writing, message after message from the very same evening. We agreed to meet on Tuesday in the shopping centre.

I came by car from one of my sports classes and parked in the carpark. While walking to our meeting point, just outside the main entrance of the shopping centre I saw an Italian friend of mine. I sat down with him for a few minutes and explained my reason for being here, my meeting, my very first meeting with a man I had just met on Meetyourlove on Sunday.

"Would you do me a favour and tell me what you think of him when we walk by later. I will stop and say hi to you so that you can have a look at him. You can let me know via WhatsApp what your first impression is."

This is fun, I thought.

So, I went to meet Oliver, at the main entrance. Right at this moment and after long grey days and the storm, the sun came out in shining glory. He was standing there, to my left, looking for me and when I approached and said with some hesitation, "Hi, Oliver?", a big smile grew on his face and his eyes sparkled. He was extremely good looking, I liked him at first sight. The sun was gleaming on his face and his body. He was tall, slim and sporty. My heart was beating very fast.

"Nice meeting you! I was so curious! After our six hours on the phone, I was curious to meet the woman in person!"

"Me too, I was curious to meet you!"

We walked by my friend, who was in a restaurant, greeted him 'by chance' and went to the nearby Asian restaurant, to eat 'Red Chicken' with rice. During our meal, my Italian friend sent me a WhatsApp message saying that he liked this man and that he was never wrong in his judgement of people.

We spent two hours having a very nice lunch together, talking, eating and drinking. Oliver invited me to his house the coming Sunday, first for a bike ride and then cooking together.

We left the shopping centre and went back to our lives. We continued exchanging many messages every day, starting in the early morning and continuing all day long until just before going to sleep. I sent countless smileys, with probably just as many hearts, and also photos of myself.

The Friday of that week was Valentine's Day and he sent me a nice video and I sent him a digital red rose. But he didn't invite me for dinner, nor anything else – no real roses, nothing. He spent the evening with his children. "Interesting," I thought. He didn't call me either. He only sent WhatsApp messages.

My friends asked me about him.

"How did it go? Did it all go well?"

"How was your first meeting?"

"When will you meet again?"

Excited, I told them, "He has invited me to his place on Sunday afternoon."

On Saturday morning, I went to teach a sports class and, on my way back, I met a very old friend in the park, out walking his dog with another friend who lived in the same town as Oliver. Naturally, I told them all about my Meetyourlove encounter and that tomorrow we would be meeting again and that I was very happy. The sun was shining in the park, the fountain was spraying water that sparkled in the sunshine and there was a sensation of spring in the air. I was excited and happy. I felt light and young, feeling the spring. On my bike, I drove back home to have lunch. I arrived home and I was just in my entrance hall, when I got Oliver's message.

I couldn't believe my eyes.

Oliver: "Hello Julia, I don't want to hurt you in any way but I am having doubts. I noticed that I am not yet ready for a new relationship. You, being such an open, charming and friendly person, you opened my eyes and showed me that I am not ready yet. I see that I am still in love with my last girlfriend and that I am incapable of letting her go. I am honest and straight and wanted to tell you this without wishing to hurt you. Therefore, I would like to postpone our meeting tomorrow to a later date. I hope you can understand me. You are a wonderful person. I can imagine very well a friendship with you. Please don't be angry with me. Kind regards. Oliver."

Me: "Can I call you to talk about this?"

Oliver: "Please could we phone in the next days, at the moment I do not really want to talk. Please do not misunderstand me. I need the time and space for me. This has nothing to do with you, but more with my coming to terms with my past. I hope you understand."

Me: "Dear Oliver, I respect you. You may call or write when you are ready. I am always here for you. Whenever you are ready. I really started liking you."

Me: "It has not been easy for me either. If you change your mind the weather is wonderful, just come to town and we'll go for a bike ride and you will feel better right away."

Oliver: "You are sweet! But I prefer to be on my own at the moment, it has absolutely nothing to do with you. It's my life and interests that I need to focus on. Therefore, no harm and hurt feelings please."

Oliver: "Thank you for understanding me."

Me: "No worries. The weather is fantastic. We could have gone cycling. We still could. If you change your mind, you can come into town tomorrow afternoon and we'll go cycling together. Only cycling, and nothing else."

Me: "Think it over one night and reply tomorrow."

Oliver: "Ok, I will think it over, but the weather may not agree with the plan…"

Me: "If it rains, we could still go for a walk in the city and have a tea somewhere. You think it over."

Oliver: "Will do. And thanks again for being so thoughtful!"

On Sunday morning, I went to teach a fitness class and kept thinking about what kind of response Oliver would give me. I was convinced he would agree to go riding and this is exactly what happened.

Oliver: "Isn't it too windy for bicycling today?"

Me: "I have to give my university lecture now but after I will go biking from here. You are welcome to join if you want. I will not ride fast and for no longer than two hours."

Oliver: "What time?"

Me: "Two thirty at my place, dressed in bike wear. Racing bike."

Oliver: "Three would be earliest I could do."

Me: "Three is perfect."

Oliver: "Ok."

We rode our bikes a good fifty or so kilometres from my place to Mersch and back on the cycle path. We also took some photos on the way and stopped off at the top of the outdoor lift in Paffendal which is a nice place for photos. The wind was mostly behind us and quite strong and so on our way we could go really fast and raced one another to see who was the swifter. The many Sunday walkers with their dogs eventually put an end to our speed.

It was a wonderful Sunday together. When we arrived back at his car, I helped to put his bike back in his car.

Oliver said, "And now, what are the plans?"

"After yesterday's experience," I replied, "I suggest you just go back home and we will meet another time."

I added, "Oliver, I am sorry. I didn't want to scare you by writing too many messages, too many smileys, too many photos. You can be sure that I am not going to bed with all the men I know. I didn't want to scare you, I am sorry, I messed it all up."

Oliver: "No, you didn't. It's okay. It's just me."

Me: "I really liked you from the first moment I saw you. We could be friends. That would be wonderful!"

Oliver drove away.

Later that evening he sent me a message thanking me for "the wonderful bike tour" and adding: "I thoroughly enjoyed it!"

I messaged back: "The pleasure was all mine. Hopefully we can go on more of them."

"Yes."

My friends all wanted to know how the Sunday with Oliver had been and I told them about our bike ride.

They asked, "When will you meet again?"

I said, "I don't know."

Over the following days we wrote. We wrote many, many messages every day. There were no further invitations from his side. There were no phone calls either. I even started asking him out, asking to meet him at a Saturday night carnival party or for a Sunday afternoon together. But he was 'occupied'.

My friends started saying, "You can forget about him. For sure he has loads of women at the same time on Meetyourlove and he gets to choose." The days went on and nothing, no invitation, literally nothing. Finally, I told my friends, "You are right, he is not interested. He almost certainly has found somebody else."

Agnès and Petra encouraged me to continue searching, not to give up and not to get fixated too much on one person but to remain open and to keep looking for other men.

Agnès insisted, "You need to continue on Meetyourlove. You'll find the right person. Don't get enthusiastic too early! Don't think it's the right man too early. Continue searching. There is a rare gem somewhere, you only need to find him. You need to keep at it. Don't give up. My daughter also needed many months and a few men. She lost many weeks because of a man who said he was divorced but was lying, he was still married. And she had to try different men, go out for lunch or a drink or a dinner with them, and do these things on different occasions. She showed us their pictures and we talked about them. And then she found her rare gem. You will do the same. It will take time. Be patient!"

One Sunday morning after teaching a fitness class I had a nap and was lying by the television watching Jessica Fletcher on 'Murder she Wrote' when Oliver texted "4 pm tea?"

I was so surprised that at first I didn't believe my eyes. Then, I didn't understand. Finally, I replied, "Where?"

"Old Sheffield's Pub."

"Ok, come to my place, park your car here and we go together from here."

"Ok"

Oliver came to my place. He rang my doorbell. I opened the main entrance door for him with the buzzer. I invited him in to see my apartment. He hesitated, he wanted to wait outside and not come in. I am sure he was also told that on these dating platforms it is better to be safe and not to meet in the home of the person but rather in a neutral place like a bar, a pub or a restaurant. You never know what kind of person your date might be.

That's certainly true.

But I insisted and said, "Please come in!"

Oliver's first reaction was, "This is Villa Kunterbunt and you are Pippi Longstocking!"

"Exactly!" I said, "Pippi is my big role model, she always was. In my childhood I read all her books and watched all her films and saw her as my hero. I always wanted to be like her, revolutionary, extra strong and helping the weak and poor."

"Oh my God, it is all so colourful here," said Oliver, "look at all your scarves! At my house, it's all empty. I have thrown away everything. My house is completely empty."

It was raining cats and dogs, but we still walked to Sheffield's Pub in the Grund district. There was a cosy table that was free and we put our shoes to dry on the radiators. We sat there the rest of the afternoon and well into the evening, talking mainly about his life. Oliver told me about his job, his life, his ex-wife and his children. I told him that I often do a SWOT analysis with my students. He said that he had never written down his own SWOT. I suggested I could do his and so we got some paper from the barmaid. It took hours. He told me everything in detail while I took notes and filled more than ten pages. When we were finished, I put all the papers together and in order for him.

"This is the first time that I have done a SWOT in my life," Oliver said.

I replied, "You know, I have an idea. I will write a book about my encounters and experiences with meeting men on Meetyourlove. Do you want to help me with the writing?"

"Well, why not. But I am not a good writer. Actually, I don't really write that much."

"You could dictate it to me and I would write it down on the computer. You could tell me the story of how we met, from your point of view."

"Let's see if we could meet again next Sunday."

"In the meantime, I will start writing my book."

Indeed, I actually started writing this book, as you can see.

We walked back to his car, which was parked in front of my apartment.

I turned to him and said, "I just wanted to say that I am sorry for having written such childish messages with all those smileys. It is not my habit to go to bed first thing with the men I meet. I wanted to say that I really liked you from the first moment and that whatever the outcome of our meeting will be, there are no coincidences in life. There is a reason why we met. Will it be a long-lasting friendship? Will it be more? I wanted to say that I really liked you from the beginning."

"I felt the same way", replied Olivier, "do you really think this was not a coincidence?"

"No, our meeting was not a coincidence. There is a reason for us meeting on Meetyourlove."

"I was not on Meetyourlove, I was on MeetLoveNow."

"You see!"

During the week, we continued exchanging messages and sending photos. But again, there were no phone calls, no invitations or offers, absolutely nothing concrete.

Then, on Wednesday evening, I came back utterly exhausted from teaching three hours in a row of sports as well as two hours of languages, and I got a message from Oliver.

"I only want to be friends with you."

Upset and tired, and also feeling fed up with the situation, I replied, "That's Ok with me."

He continued by writing, "I wanted to be with other people!"

"What kind of people?"

"Other people in general!"

"Ok"

"NOT with you!" wrote Oliver, "I don't want to be with you. I want to be with everyday people."

Okay, I thought, this is a psycho case. Maybe he is bipolar or manic depressive, or he is just crazy, completely crazy. I don't need this, especially not at nine thirty in the evening after a long and exhausting day of teaching. There are good manners and ways of saying things and there is the right time for saying the important things.

I didn't even reply.

The next day, I told my friends about this incident. They suggested I block him as a contact. That's exactly what I did.

Anyhow, this is not the end of this story, because even if you block contacts on your mobile phone, they re-appear, somehow....

Luca

I found this man on Meetyourlove. His name was Luca and he seemed to be Italian. I contacted him through the site on a rainy Sunday afternoon. He answered my first contact request and I gave him my telephone number. He called me just a few minutes later.

After a few minutes introducing ourselves, I asked him where he lived and discovered that his place was only a few minutes by bike from my place. So, I suggested we stop talking on the phone and meet in person. On his Meetyourlove page, under the question "Lives with?", he had written "I live in a shared household." Well, I thought, who might this be? When I arrived with my bike at his house, he told me who was sharing his house with: his mother! He is of Italian origin but didn't speak Italian particularly well and preferred sticking to English all the time. We met around six o'clock and went for a walk through town. It was drizzling with the everyday Luxembourgish light rain – grey, dark, and continuous. After our walk, we went for a drink.

During the whole time we were together he spoke. He spoke and spoke and spoke. Without ever stopping. I didn't say a word, or close to nothing. From six onwards, he spoke without a break. It was like a monologue, no, it was a real, genuine monologue. I didn't add anything to his talk. Eventually, at around seven thirty, I had finished drinking my non-alcoholic beer but he was still sipping his. I looked pointedly at the clock on his mobile phone and said, "Oh, it's already half past seven. I am sorry, I have to go home to work some more." He replied, "That's perfect, let's go. My mother is waiting with dinner for me!"

I said, "We could remain friends."

He replied, "Oh no, I don't need more friends. I am not on Meetyourlove to make new friends. I already have enough friends. I have been on Meetyourlove for years and always find a new girlfriend on this platform. Through Meetyourlove I have already found two girlfriends in the last few years. So, no, I am looking for a girlfriend, not for more friends."

All the way back he talked and talked and talked, almost without even pausing for breath. I had not uttered one single sentence about myself for the last hour or so and when I came back home I was exhausted from the noise and happy to be alone. Hopefully, I will not hear anymore from him, but who knows, maybe one day...he will be there to talk and talk and talk...

Some phone calls

There was one Sunday evening that I got quite a few phone calls from men contacted on Meetyourlove. I had sent them a contact message with my phone number. Therefore, they called me. This is the best and easiest way of not wasting time.

Apparently, the usual contact procedure is for people to write messages on Meetyourlove, many messages over weeks, before they exchange phone numbers to get to talk directly. For me, this is a waste of time. If I want to know if somebody could interest me, I find it best to get to speak to them first on the phone. If a person seems suitable then the next step would be a meeting in person. That is why I prefer sharing my phone number directly, to save time.

On this Sunday evening, one of these men called. We had been talking for around two or three minutes, when he said in a friendly but firm manner "I think, honestly, we do not have so many things in common! This was a nice conversation and you are a nice person but we will not go any further. I thank you for your time, for the nice talk and wish you all the best with your search for a partner. Thank you and good evening." During the weeks that followed I had many such phone calls. I was happy to have them as they saved me precious time.

Mike

"Interesting", I thought while looking at his photo, "He looks interesting."

"Good looking, smiling, and standing on his boat," I continued thinking.

"Well, give him my phone number and we'll speak."

Indeed, just a few minutes after having sent my number in the Meetyourlove message, he called me. "Hello, is your name really Julia?" he asked. We had a nice phone call.

"I used to exercise a lot, like you," Mike informed me, "but now I have problems with my knees, I cannot run any more, nor can I go skiing, or cycling. It simply hurts too much. That's why I changed my job. I am not teaching sports or exercising any longer."

I thought, "Oh no! That's not what I am looking for."

"What about meeting in person?" he asked.

"Good idea!"

"I'll treat you to dinner in a nice restaurant", he offered and continued, "I often have lunch and dinner with friends and family. I like eating and drinking out. I like wine."

I thought, "Oh, no, I don't drink. I don't drink any alcohol. This is not the right man for me. But anyhow, who knows, let's give it a try."

On the day of our dinner, I had to pull out because of work. I was not feeling particularly romantic or talkative, instead, I simply wrote, "Sorry, I have to cancel our dinner, I have to work."

Two days later he wrote, "Do you not want to meet at all?"

I agreed to meet the following Saturday in a place of his choosing. We didn't write or exchange any messages during the week until Thursday, when he wrote:

"It is not conventional or traditional, but I want to ask you if you would come with me to a private dinner at a friend's house on Saturday evening. If you can be so spontaneous?"

"Yes, I am spontaneous," I agreed, "and yes I will go with you. What shall I bring?"

He said, "There are eight of us. I'll take care of everything."

"Please remember that I don't drink any alcohol," I replied, "and please I don't want to stay late because I am working the next morning."

"No problem, we will not make it late night," said Mike.

I asked him what type of car he was coming to pick me up with and where the house was we were going to.

As promised, on Saturday, he came to pick me up at seven thirty and we drove to his friend's house. In the car, we talked about his profession and he told me about what he was doing. I asked my questions and he gave his answers.

I listened very carefully, following the good advice of my friends.

He told me, somewhat self-importantly, "I have reduced my professional activity on purpose because I have enough money and enough wealth to live on. I have no need to work for a living." He added proudly, "I can live without having to work, and I can live well."

"Lucky him!" I thought, "that's not really the case with me."

After this informative drive, we arrived at his friend's house.

I thought, "This is not my cup of tea and it's going to be a complete waste of time."

Mike had two boxes of red wine for the evening in the boot of his car together with a bouquet of white tulips. He gave these to me to hand over to the friend's wife.

Not for me, no, for the friend's wife... ok.

The evening went quite well. They all talked Luxembourgish and were all native Luxembourgers. The house was very nice, very expensive and very beautiful, everything was the best. We talked about kitchens, furniture, cars and about wine. The 'woman of the house' was very kind but seemed to have nothing to say. She prepared some warm starters and she also prepared dinner.

By around ten, the meal was not ready yet and so I asked, in a friendly but determined manner, "Do you think, it would be possible to be home by eleven as I have to work tomorrow."

They looked at me in horror.

"I thought we would make it three or four in the morning?" Mike said.

I replied, "No, normally I go to bed at ten when I work in the mornings although sometimes, I make an exception. Eleven is late for me but it's okay. Do you think you could drive me home and then you can come back to the party?"

They must have thought that I was completely boring and absolutely out of my mind.

They looked at me with astonishment and in disbelief.

"How come you go to bed so early on a Saturday evening?"

"Why do you not drink red wine?"

"Why on earth are you not interested in furniture?"

Finally, we sat down to eat our chili con carne. It was a quarter past ten and I had the very clear impression that it was only for me that they had started eating 'so early'.

They continued drinking red wine, a lot of red wine. And talking about furniture. They showed each other photos of their precious pieces on their smart phones. They talked about the furniture fairs they had attended and intended to go to in the future. This is not exactly the subject I am most interested in.

Mike helped himself to a second dish of chili con carne and said to me, "I'll eat this and will drive you home."

Finally, I said goodbye to everybody very kindly and he drove me home. It was a cold, damp and dark evening, as is often the case in Luxembourg. He put on the seat heating in his car for me.

By this time, it was eleven thirty and I fell asleep in his car before even getting to my place. He had to wake me up when he stopped in front of my door.

I said goodbye, thanked him kindly for the evening, excused myself for sleeping and away I went.

He must have thought that I was such a boring person. I don't drink alcohol. I don't talk about furniture. I don't do late nights. I go to sleep early. I work on Sunday mornings. I have to work for my living. He is wealthy enough not to work. How boring I must have seemed to him.

It was not a 'successful evening', an absolute disaster in fact!

On 7 March 2020, the first case of coronavirus appeared in Luxembourg.

Christophe

He was skiing somewhere and wrote a message in reply to me contacting him.

He wrote, "I will contact you when I get back from my skiing vacation. I cannot write or telephone now from here because I have no privacy at the moment, being together with friends."

He also wrote on Meetyourlove, as a reply to my question to call via WhatsApp or Skype or anything else other than the usual telephone, "I do not use WhatsApp or Facebook or any other social media because I do not trust them."

We agreed to phone when he was back from his ski trip.

In fact, he phoned on Tuesday evening. He had been training on Monday night, and he was still aching. We talked about his cycling and he mentioned that he was in the same bike club as Carl.

Christophe said, "Carl is a very kind person. Once I shared a room with him on one of our bicycle trips."

That's funny. Luxembourg is small. Everybody knows everybody.

We agreed to meet for lunch on Tuesday in a week at a restaurant not so far away.

On the Tuesday, I arrived early to be able to see him arrive. I like watching people and seeing how they behave when they don't feel observed. Goes with the job, I suppose!

I waited outside near the restaurant on the sidewalk and watched everybody going into the restaurant, trying to guess if one of them was him or not. I was content to be doing my favourite sport of observing people. There was an extremely nice looking man walking up to the restaurant, looking at the door, not me, and he went straight past, and I thought, "Oh, this for sure is not him, even though it would be nice if it were."

Several other men ranging from more or less good looking to extremely unpleasant looking– at least in my eyes – went into the restaurant and I hoped that none of them was him.

Then, a man arrived on a bike and I thought, "That's him". It then took him five minutes or so – it seemed an eternity to me – to lock his bike to the fence, while I was watching him all the time.

I thought, "Oh no, this is such a slow person. Never would I want to be with him." I continued thinking, "He is not good looking either. Where are the muscles, and the strong legs, the abdominals and the cute bottom? I cannot see any of those!"

The first impression was confirmed.

We had a nice lunch. We ate our meal and talked. He told me about his studies and his work.

He told me, "It took me ten years to study for my Master's, but you need to know that I was working at the same time to finance my studies, and I was doing many other things also."

"Aha!" I replied.

He added, "You know, I am a victim of workplace bullying."

He continued by talking about his last girlfriend and the reason she left.

We eventually parted and he said he was sick, so, in times of coronavirus, we remained suitably distant.

Christophe called me the Saturday after and spent a while on the phone.

He was a nice person, a bit slow but friendly.

After this phone call, I never heard from him again.

Or at least, I thought so. Some weeks later....

Northern Italy, especially Lombardy and Milano, is greatly affected by the coronavirus, and many elderly people die from it.

Government ministers try to contain the spread of the virus with measures like closing schools, kindergartens, universities as well as cancelling flights.

For the most part, this does not have much impact, unfortunately, as the virus continues spreading.

People are told not to travel, to wash their hands, not to greet others by shaking hands, not to kiss and not to hug.

Larry

Larry had also been skiing, just like Christophe, and also preferred to write or contact me when back from holiday as he too said it was not private enough where he was. I thought he wouldn't contact me again. However, he did so after a few days.

"Hello Julia, I hope you are doing well", he messaged, "I arrived back later than expected and am in a hurry to empty my bags and wash all my stuff and I am very tired. Do you mind if we call tomorrow evening? Have a nice evening, cheers, Larry."

I answered, "Dear Larry, thank you for your kind message and I prefer talking on Tuesday or on Wednesday, if possible. Have a nice day. Julia."

He replied, "Hello Julia, I hope you are doing well. Yes of course, no problem. Let's talk on Wednesday evening if that suits you. Have a great day. Larry."

On the Wednesday evening, I was worn out from teaching five hours in a row. When I arrived back home on my bike, with the rain, the cold and the darkness, there were the messages from Oliver saying he only wanted to be friends and not wanting to see me at all. And there was this long message from Larry.

"Dear Julia! I hope you are doing well! I just got back home. Just before I call you, I just want to be honest with you. At the moment, I have a lot of new projects which take a lot of time, meaning being home late every day over the coming months. Second, I told you I am going to move house in four months. I still have to pack everything over the next twelve weekends. ... So, I am very busy and that might not be what you are looking for. It doesn't mean I have no time, but I don't have much time. For my previous girlfriend that was a no-go, which I fully understand. If you have the same opinion, no problem, we might try to call later this year (or not at all). If you could take it into account, we can still call tonight. Just don't want to waste your (and my) time. Just let me know and I will (or will not) call you."

We arranged to call at that very moment.

It was a nice call, after all.

We managed to arrange a dinner together on Saturday night. The next day, I had to ask him to change the plan for another day, as I was busy on Saturday night. He suggested Friday night.

Caroline's experiences

We – Caroline and I – were talking about our experiences with online dating platforms and she mentioned two in particular.

"Men are no longer dating in the streets", she said, "It is rare to see a man approach you in the street or to invite you for a drink. Most of them don't dare to do this anymore. They are on online dating platforms."

"Some time ago, I was also dating on a dating platform and I had several men that I was chatting with at the same time. Most of us do so, I think, chatting with several people in parallel. This seems to be normal to me."

She continued, "There was however one man who literally shocked me, I will never forget the sentence he wrote to me. While chatting with a few men at once it took me a bit of time to reply to each post. Apparently, he was impatient and wouldn't wait. Suddenly, I read 'Va te faire foutre sale pute.' – 'F*** you, you dirty whore.' This was really disgusting to me. I was completely shocked and I blocked the contact directly."

"Another meeting was just as incredible", she went on, "In Thionville there is this tower in the town centre, I don't know if it still exists, with a bar and restaurant at the top. This man I was in contact with was giving himself airs, especially linguistic airs. When writing and speaking, he used a language that was so high and so snobbish, it was strange to me. He pretended to like only well-styled and well-dressed women of a certain class. So, I was really curious to get to know this person. I always arrive early to these appointments, so I can observe the person on arrival. I was standing so he couldn't see me. He arrived in an old Renault Clio, which didn't match the high airs he was giving himself. Then I saw him lowering the mirror in the car and checking his looks. I saw him putting perfume on, this was hilarious. He perfumed all over. Later at the bar, we ordered champagne. I spotted immediately that he didn't know anything about champagne but only affected to know. He pretended the champagne we were drinking was excellent, even though it obviously wasn't. I know champagne and wine and I can drink a lot before showing it, so I put together a plan. I would drink him under the table and he would be punished for all the women he has mistreated this way. So, we ordered a red wine and another red wine and again. He commented on how high quality this wine was, which it wasn't. Then he said that he likes women dressed in stockings, stockings made with a special material. I thought, you idiot, I will have you. I quickly made up the name of a German lingerie brand. 'Yes,' I said, 'I always wear Weinberg stockings.' And this idiot replied 'Excellent choice! Absolutely excellent!' By this time, he was starting to feel the effects of the alcohol and I asked for another glass, just to get revenge. He had to pay for all these drinks, and he did pay."

"That was the experience. Never heard from the man again. Didn't want to either."

LOCKED DOWN LOVE

Alan

"How was your evening?" Alan asked me.

"Oh, that was, I mean, uhm, well, let's put it this way, it was a free dinner and also a free lunch, as I only ate half of the lasagne yesterday evening and the leftovers today for lunch."

"But the man?"

"I think I will not hear from him anymore."

"Why?"

"Because, well I think, I was not his type. He must have thought that I was completely nuts. All the time he was looking at me with this weird astonishment in his face. I seemed not to be his kind of woman."

"Ai!"

"However, I learned a lot about social behaviour. He told me about his former Luxembourgish girlfriend. She was so typically Luxembourgish, like some Germans or Dutch people. Uncertainty Avoidance 100%. She needed to plan everything. No surprises. No unexpected moments. No improvisation. Every weekend was meant to be for them as a couple. Every weekend and every Tuesday and Thursday evening. Not Monday or Wednesday. No. Tuesday evening and Thursday evening. Without ever deviating from this unwritten rule. Very Luxembourgish. They need to know what they will be doing on the third Tuesday in October in three years from now. Otherwise, they feel uncomfortable."

"Completely the opposite of me, if I know exactly what I am going to be doing next weekend, I am depressed."

"And then they spoke only Luxembourgish when they were among family and friends. They would translate a summary for him. This was getting in the way of communication."

"I know this feeling."

"Besides, he hated going for a walk in these small Luxembourgish villages every Saturday and Sunday, with the dog, always at the same time and always the same routes. He was getting horribly bored."

"Like this couple that I see every morning walking their dog in front of my house at five past seven. Never six past seven, no, always five past, whatever the weather. She always walks in front on the sidewalk, holding the dog on the leash walking behind her and after the dog walks the husband. I suppose that the dog is also bored with always taking the same walk at the same time every day."

Alan then decided it was high time to give me some advice and said, "Anyway Julia, you have to pay attention, there are a lot of fake profiles on these dating sites. Especially, there are many women who are not women, but men. I know this for a fact because a few years back, for a joke, a friend and me, we created a profile of a woman to get to one of our friends. We knew his username and found him. We contacted him, as a woman, and started a conversation with him. After a while, we revealed our true identity. We all had a good laugh!"

"You pay attention, Julia," he added, "and you'll be fine. This is better than being sad. Don't cry any longer. Please. Maybe one day, you will really find a treasure there on the platform or elsewhere. I will always love you, but I love my new girlfriend more. You and I had wonderful years, the best experiences of my life, they are unforgettable. You gave me everything I ever dreamt of, but I love another woman now. Don't cry, I am still here, we will remain good friends."

Jordan

"This year, climate change has been put aside for coronavirus," Jordan said.

We were discussing politics, a subject dear to his heart.

"Everything's only about coronavirus nowadays, twenty-four hours a day, seven days a week. There seems to be nothing else but coronavirus. They seem to have forgotten about all the other issues, like climate change, global warming, rising sea levels, the melting of glaciers, and Islamic State, radical Islamism, and the protection of nature!"

"By the way, have you seen all the cigarette butts here on this parking spot! Let me pick them up so I can throw them away in the bin."

Louis

Louis and I have been friends for years. Now that I was dating on Meetyourlove, I learned that Louis was also a single man again. Single because his girlfriend had left him. At Carnival time earlier in the year, Louis had invited all of us to a wonderful party over at his house. We danced and he taught us Zumba dances. I came disguised in a brown short-haired wig. Louis was fascinated.

He said, "Oh, I like you as brown-haired girl. I cannot stand blondes anymore. Please be a brunette always!"

He said this because the girlfriend who had betrayed him was also blonde and his ex-wife as well. Despite the jokes, I saw the sadness in Louis's eyes.

Sometime later, I called him and said, "Louis, I have been left by my boyfriend and have been very lonely and very sad, I see you are in the same boat: lonely and sad. A friend of mine suggested that I should register at Meetyourlove, the online dating platform, and honestly, since I am on Meetyourlove the sadness has gone. I am occupied. I don't always have great meetings or find the best guys, but it keeps me busy and I forget about my sadness and my loneliness. You should try it also."

"Why not?" answered Louis.

"Especially," I said, "since the two of us cannot be together. It would not be good for our reputations. Nor can we try all of our participants in the sports classes."

Louis countered, "Ah, but if I meet you on Meetyourlove, then we could go out together!?!? This is a wonderful idea. We'll try dating other people on Meetyourlove and if at the end of this year, we haven't found anybody, then the two of us can come together!"

"Ok, that's a deal!"

March, 2020. *Many more cases of coronavirus in Luxembourg.*

The company where I am teaching language classes put in place an emergency plan for coronavirus. Teams and people were designated as being able to work from home or not.

Quick adventures, photos, phone calls and other men

Not surprisingly, there were those men on Meetyourlove who were after a quick adventure, mainly in bed. They would WhatsApp me their nude and semi-nude pictures asking for the same kind in return, which I never sent, of course.

Others called me and after around five minutes they would say, "Thank you, this was a nice conversation but we do not really fit together. Thank you and all the best for you. I wish you a nice day/afternoon/evening."

Ackim

February, 2020.

"Hello AK, how are you? What is your real name? Achim? Have a nice day. Julia."

"Hello Julia, how are you? Not far off with Achim, at least the "A" was correct :). My name is Ackim or Aky for short. Curious to know how you made the association with Achim, though. You have an exceptional profile and all that with a bit of humour. Looking forward to exchanging further."

"Hello Aky, if you wish, we could telephone, 00352.611.111.111. Julia."

"Hello Julia, a call would be lovely. What are convenient times? By the way I sent you a LinkedIn invitation. Should give me some further insights into the woman :))"

"Dear Aky, I accepted your LinkedIn invitation. You could call me today at nine tonight, if you have time. Otherwise tomorrow morning before eleven. It would be my pleasure to talk to you. Speak to you later. Am teaching some more lessons. Julia."

"Hello Julia, I tried reaching you but to no availability. Do not hesitate to call me on 811.111.111. Speak to you soon. Aky."

So, one Thursday morning in February, I took my phone and called Aky. It was a quarter to nine in the morning. He answered with a brief "Hello".

"Hello, this is Julia".

"Oh, Julia, hello, nice to speak to you. I tried calling you yesterday evening but you didn't reply."

"Well, I was already sleeping."

"I am in the car now, on my way to Switzerland, for skiing. I took a long weekend to go skiing. And after that I will be travelling for my company to Denmark, to France and to London."

"You can write me and send me pictures and we also could phone."

"At nine my office will call me for a conference call."

"Ah, that's very soon. We will talk later. Do you know that I am teaching at your former employer?"

"Oh really, are you? We'll talk about this later. Lovely talking to you and I'll send photos, even though I am not photogenic."

At eleven, I went to teach my language class and asked my student, "Do you remember Aky?"

He replied, "Yes, of course. We used to work together for years. Why?" He looked at me with a questioning look on his face and then seeing my smile, he asked, "Don't tell me that you have met him on Meetyourlove?"

I replied, "Yes, I have met him on Meetyourlove."

"What kind of man is he?" I wanted to know.

He answered, "I knew him only professionally. He is a nice person. Sometimes a bit ambitious and he can be nervous. Once, I had to tell him to sit down when he was pacing up and down the conference room endlessly. I told him, 'now Aky you sit down and we'll talk, you make me all worried with your walking around.'"

I asked, "What do you think about him and me... together?"

He looked at me and said, "Give it a try."

"Shall we write to him now? What do you think? We'll write to him together."

"We'll send him a picture of us!"

And so, I wrote a WhatsApp message to Aky, sending him our photo.

Aky replied directly, he was having lunch at the ski resort and was very happy to see us.

He replied, "It seems that I need some polishing, with a woman like you!"

This made me smile.

During the day, he sent more pictures from the ski resort.

We phoned the same evening and phoned more often in the following days. Long phone calls. Very nice long phone calls. Mostly I was in bed when we talked.

We also wrote WhatsApp messages. Many messages. Many photos.

After the ski weekend, he drove back to Luxembourg but it was too late in the evening when he got home and I was too tired. Aky asked me if we could meet on Monday evening but I really was too tired.

Aky then travelled to his various destinations. He sent photos and text messages and we phoned. We got used to writing in the early mornings before work and during the evenings after work. We often phoned at night and talked.

While Aky was waiting to board his plane to Luxembourg on a Sunday in March, he wrote that he was kicking his heels at the airport and asked how I was. I replied and we continued writing many messages, until his plane started boarding. He finished up with, "Now we are boarding, talk to you soon."

On the Monday, there was a full moon, and I called him, "Good evening Aky, am I disturbing you?"

"No, otherwise I would not have answered the phone. However, it is quite cold here."

We talked for a long while on the phone, me lying in bed, him standing in the cold in Limpertsberg in front of a café. After a while, and since he was not taking the initiative, I asked, "So, when will we meet?"

We agreed to meet at a restaurant not far from my apartment on Friday the thirteenth. "Well," I said, "that's a nice day. Should bring luck."

Aky said, "I will come to pick you up at your place at seven thirty.

We continued the conversation by talking about the coronavirus.

I told him that I was afraid of losing my classes and "if they cancel the classes, if they close the schools, and sports halls, how will I earn money?" I had already discussed this with other people and everybody said the same: 'we keep our heads up high and will fight this difficult time with pride. We will not let it get us down. No.'

"With rising temperatures later in the year, the virus will disappear just like the flu," he assured me.

As for my money woes, he said, "You should do more online teaching via Skype or WhatsApp."

That was a very wise suggestion.

Tuesday, 10 March 2020

- *In Italy, the entire country was under coronavirus lockdown.*

- *Schools were closed. Universities closed.*

- *Later, airports would be shut down worldwide.*

- *Tourist trips were cancelled.*

- *Ski resorts were closed.*

- *Stock markets experienced sharp falls.*

- *The crude oil price fell thirty percent and then more.*

- *People bought toilet paper, disinfectant, noodles and rice.*

- *Supermarkets were emptied.*

- *People were asked to remain home.*

- *People were asked not to travel, to wash their hands, not to greet others by shaking hands, not to kiss and not to hug.*

- *The travel ban was extended to cover nearly everybody.*

- *Restaurants remained empty and lifeless. People were afraid of catching the virus.*

- *It was recommended to remain two meters from other people, which is impossible in most places.*

- *Cinemas, theatres and all public places closed.*

- *Services for subways, buses and trams were cut back or cancelled.*

- *The entire public life came to a standstill.*

- *All big events were cancelled.*

- *Football matches were without spectators.*

- *The Milano–San Remo bike race was cancelled.*

- *The Leipziger Book Fair was cancelled.*

Carl

Thursday, 12 March 2020

Just before my sports class started, Carl called me.

He asked, "How are you? Do you still have your sports classes? What will happen, when you will not have your classes anymore? Do you need financial help? Please tell me, if you need my help. Please, in case the authorities close schools, sport halls, what will you do? How can I help you, financially and morally?"

I answered, "I really hope they do not close the sports halls, because then I will not earn any more money. How shall we all survive? It is horrible. What shall we live from? I am an independent worker, you know that, no money comes in when I do not work, if I do not teach my classes, what shall I live from?"

"There should be a State solution," he reassured me, "a decision by the government to help the independent people so they can survive this difficult time. You should write an email to our mayor, to ask her for help."

Later, Aky and I had a long call in the evening, talking about the events of the day.

Alan sent me Viber messages.

"I think a lot about our cycling holidays and about the good times we had together", he wrote, adding "After this epidemic, nothing will be the same."

He finished by saying, "I miss you, you will always be my Julia!"

Friday, 13 March 2020

One could say this was a real Friday the thirteenth.

In Luxembourg, all the schools and sports halls and many other places were closed for the next three weeks at least. This meant that I would not have any classes to teach for at least five weeks. What's more, the company where I teach language lessons wouldn't let anybody in for the coming weeks.

In the morning, I got a phone call telling me, "The sports hall is now closed. We have just locked it up. As a result, there will be no sports class tonight. Please inform your students."

I went to teach my in-house company language class. I told my students, "This will be the last lesson we will be having together for a while. Please stay healthy and please continue learning your language, otherwise you forget everything." One student already was participating via a conference call, as he was working from home. The company had installed a plan for remote working to ensure business continuity.

After this last class, I went for a jog, I was really sad. This is awful. What's happening to us is absolutely horrible. I was running in tears, when the phone rang. It was Carl.

"How are you, Julia?"

"I am crying, jogging and trying to forget. Trying to cope with this new situation. How shall we survive? What shall we live from? No teaching! No income!"

"What are you doing tomorrow? Do you want to go cycling together?"

"Yes, with pleasure. When? Where to?"

"In the afternoon, after lunch, the weather is going to be very sunny and warm. We could go to Clémency. I will write to you and let you know when exactly, but I'll be at your place around three in the afternoon."

"Ok, that will be lovely."

In the evening, Aky and I met for the first time in person. I had been nervous about meeting him ever since we had agreed on the date. What to wear? How to do my hair?

We had agreed via WhatsApp that he would come to my place to pick me up at seven thirty from my place and then walk to the restaurant.

At seven thirty, he called and asked, "Where are you? I am standing outside the restaurant and waiting for you and you are not here."

I said, "Ah, ok, I thought we had agreed on you coming to my place. No problem, give me a second, and I will be there."

Strange, I thought.

I hurried to get my coat and shoes and went down the street.

Then he was standing in front of me. I thought, this is a kind person.

We spent an enjoyable evening together at the restaurant. It was one of the last evenings it was to be open. Also, we didn't shake hands, we didn't hug, nor approach one another, just sat at the table and talked and ate our delicious dinner. There was so much to talk about. We took pictures, I always take pictures of everything. He kept saying, "I am not photogenic. I am an old man. I feel like an old man, while you are a young lady."

We took some more pictures and he continued by saying, "You look much younger than me." Actually, it is the other way around and he is a couple of years younger than me.

After dinner, we walked back to his car. Despite coronavirus, we kissed on the cheek. Maybe we should not have done this. We also should have stayed two meters apart to prevent transmission of the virus. We didn't stick to this rule either. This was not good.

The same evening, Carl sent some WhatsApp messages.

Alan wrote some more Viber messages.

Carl

Saturday, 14 March 2020

In the morning, I taught my language class online via a conference call with my favourite student.

I just had time to have a quick lunch and change for the ride with Carl. He arrived under my balcony with his bike, in the sun, while I was washing the dishes, I heard the spinning of his bike wheels between the bird song. I shouted out from my kitchen, "Hello Carl!"

He replied, "Hello Julia!"

I stepped out onto the balcony into the sun. There he was standing, smiling and out of breath from the ride. He looked very good. He looked happy to see me.

We were heading to Clémency. It was a warm, sunny day after months of rain and grey, and despite, or maybe especially because of the coronavirus crisis, we really enjoyed biking in the sunshine. We talked. As always, Carl talked a lot. He always has to tell me a lot and is usually very chatty. There were road works on the cycle path and officially it was closed to pedestrians and cyclists. We ignored this and climbed over the fence with our bikes and rode down the muddy path. We arrived at Clémency train station. Normally, it is a restaurant and bar but it was closed for the duration of the crisis. We stayed for a bit under the roof of the terrace and talked.

He looked at me and said, "Your hair is so beautiful!"

"Oh, thank you!" I said and blushed.

We stood in the sun and talked and talked.

Around seven that evening, Carl said good-bye, "See you tomorrow, if you are available in the afternoon. I could come around the same time, between two and three."

"Yes, bye-bye, see you tomorrow. Tomorrow afternoon, I will be going for a walk with Jordan and Jasmine. Please text me, so that I can let you know when we are back. This will be a bit later, around four, as we will be walking in Bambesch at two."

Aky

Just after Carl had left, I had to get ready urgently. I had asked Aky for a walk and he was arriving in thirty minutes.

I had asked Aky the day before to come over for a walk starting from my place. This was one of my spontaneous ideas that I often have. Some men are afraid of these spur-of-the-moment thoughts of mine while others find them funny and amusing. If he was happy about the invitation, I will never know. He accepted and he came.

He called from his phone to tell me that he had arrived, instead of ringing my doorbell.

"Ok", I thought, "This is new and strange, but well, every person has their own habits."

"I am outside, in front of your door. Where can I put my bike?"

"Just a second, I am coming down," I replied.

He was standing there on the sidewalk with his bike. It was raining but not heavily, just the typical Luxembourg light rain.

I said, "Let's put the bike in the courtyard so that nobody will steal it."

His bike chain was rusty from his last ride because of the salt from the gritting of the snow and ice on the road. As we went to the courtyard, he told me that he had not used his bike for a while and the chain had rusted. I suggested that we clean his bike so that he could get home safely.

We went for a walk, while discussing the state of the world. Aky repeated what he already had told me the evening before at the restaurant and on the phone during the last two weeks, "I feel like an old man. You are a young woman. I am an old man."

He added, "I am a practicing catholic. When I was young, I was inhibited and insecure. Nowadays this has changed and I am working on myself. I am working on my passion, and passions. Also, I pray, I have a daily prayer I say several times a day. There is a lot I have to work on, especially on passion."

"Look. This is the prayer, see here on my smartphone."

I replied, "I am practicing protestant; you are practicing catholic. There is not a big difference, however history has seen this little difference bring about wars, thousands of deaths, the division of Ireland, Northern Ireland and so on."

Aky went home at around ten thirty. It was an interesting evening. After having returned home, he wrote to thank me.

THINGS GET HECTIC

Sunday, 15 March 2020: Aky, Jordan, Carl

Aky

In Luxembourg, all restaurants, bars and pubs were closed.

Aky went golfing all day. He wrote a message early in the morning, wishing me a nice day. I am capable of reading between the lines. This meant we wouldn't speak to or see each other for the entire day. And this is exactly how it went. I did not hear from him again all day long.

The weather was very pleasant. There was a blue sky and it was warm, above twenty degrees by the afternoon.

Jordan

After lunch, I biked to Bambesch forest to meet Jordan and Jasmine for a walk. It was the time of social distancing: to stay home or to go out while staying two metres apart from each other. We went for a long two-hour walk through Bambesch and, like many of the other people there, we enjoyed the weather and took pictures of the flowers and trees.

Carl

Just as we were taking photos of an unusually shaped tree, my phone beeped. Carl had written that he would be coming to see me after my walk, if I had finished it. "Yes, I have time, I am very happy to see you," I sent back. I speeded up the pace with Jordan and Jasmine and hurried to my bike. Jordan did not understand that I had another appointment. Jasmine understood it right away and wished me luck. I told Jasmine it was one of the men I had met on Meetyourlove.

Carl came to my place, by car this time. He wanted to talk. We went for a walk. We went to the Pétrusse valley. The trees were blossoming beautifully. It was a pleasure looking at the flowers. He really had the need to talk.

He talked and I listened. He was happy with me listening to him sharing his concerns about his children.

When I had the impression he had said it all, I looked at him and said, "Feeling better?"

I told him, "Please understand me, I love you and I will always love you. But on Meetyourlove, I have met many men. There is one whom I especially like. I want to give him a chance. Also, I started writing a book."

"What kind of a book?"

"I started writing a book about my experiences with the men I met on Meetyourlove."

"Oh, looking at you and seeing that sparkling in your eyes, this must be interesting!"

"Well, yes, indeed. I have met interesting men there."

We continued walking.

Carl said, "In times of coronavirus, before we die, let me tell you, how much I love you."

"We need to be careful, not to contaminate one another. The coronavirus is terrible. We need to protect ourselves."

"Good. Do you think we will still be able to cycle tomorrow?"

"Yes, that would be nice!"

"See you tomorrow for the bike ride!"

Carl left for home and I exchanged some more messages with him, and also with Aky, Alan and Jordan.

Monday, 16 March
Alan, Carl, Aky and Jordan

We all were working from home because everything was closed because of coronavirus. I wrote messages, starting from early in the morning, to Alan, Carl, Aky and Jordan.

I asked Aky if he wanted to go for a run with me. In Luxembourg, contrary to some other countries, the lockdown rules allowed for two people to go running or cycling, provided they kept to social distancing.

We arranged to go jogging in the evening after the workday.

It was such a strange day. For coronavirus reasons almost all places were closed and all my in-presence classes had been cancelled and therefore I taught them online.

Alan

Alan called at ten in the morning and asked, "Do you have time to go cycling over lunch time? I would enjoy a bike ride together."

"Yes, with pleasure," I replied. And so, Alan came at twelve on his bike and we rode together until about two. It was a sunny day and at Dippach we sat on a bench in the sun and talked for a while.

Carl

Five minutes after getting back from the bike ride with Alan, Carl sent me a WhatsApp message, asking:

"Do you want to go cycling with me now?

"Yes, with pleasure," I agreed, even though I had just returned from a two-hour ride with Alan. Carl arrived on his bike and rang at my door. We went around town on the cycle path. The trees were continuing to blossom and the natural world was so lovely. From three until five, we talked while cycling.

Aky

At five, after arriving home, I lay down for a little nap, because after my two two-hour bike rides, I would be meeting up at six thirty with Aky for a run in the park. Luckily, I was in a good shape!

He had said to meet him at the Adolphe Bridge. Of course, he was not punctual.

At the arranged time he called and said, "I am at the Elisabeth Foundation, walking, not running."

"Ok, I'll come and meet you there!"

We met and went jogging through town and enjoyed the fine views which were bathed in a lovely sunset light. Later, they were even more stunning in the darkness.

I asked him, "Would you like to travel together?"

"Yes, if you want the company," replied Aky.

I thought this was a weird answer, but anyway.

Just for a test, I said, "After this coronavirus crises, we could travel to Australia together."

He looked at me with open eyes, as to say 'No, never!' But, okay, I understood.

What a strange day!

However, in the evening, just before going to bed, I thought, "Now I will stop asking this Aky out. It was always me who took all the initiative. This is not normal. I will stop writing and asking him out and will see what happens."

Jordan

Later, Jordan wrote a text message: "Please, I love you so much, please be part of my family. I want to marry you. We can share my children. I love you so much. Kisses. Sleep well, good night my Julia, your Jordan in love!"

Tuesday, 17 March 2020
and the following days

In Italy, the coronavirus continues to kill many people, especially in the north, in Bergamo. People die by the hundreds. It is a disaster. It makes me so sad. It makes me panic.

"We all will die," I thought.

"These are our last days. We should take advantage of life and live every minute as if it were the last."

Alan

Alan called to say, "After this coronavirus crisis, nothing will be the same. We will learn to cherish our freedom. I want to go cycling, to feel the wind in the dunes in Northern Holland, I want to make love, I want to eat out, I want to walk on the beach, to meet friends, to travel, to enjoy my liberty, the democracy we have. This is the end of Europe. The borders in Europe are re-installed. Great Britain thinks it is not concerned by the epidemic. The USA also think they are not concerned. They do nothing. This means it will be too late. They will have many dead people. Especially in the USA, where many people don't have health insurance. This is going to be dramatic. If the coronavirus hits Africa, slums in Africa, they all will die from it."

I said, "I am afraid for our lives. If we die. If I get sick, who will look after me? I am all alone!"

"You will not be sick! Never!" replied Alan, "You are so strong!"

Carl

Carl came in the afternoon, after lunch, for cycling. We enjoyed the ride very much. It was warm and sunny and we did about thirty kilometres together. We talked and took pictures. We had a break with a little picnic on a bench. We ate and drank from what we had in our backpacks. He then went back home on his own.

"Carl, I love you," I said.

He replied, "Oh, Julia, you don't know how much I love you!"

I started crying. "And if we all die? What if this is the last time we cycle together?"

"We will not die", he said, "We are too strong, too young. We still have so much energy. Heaven doesn't want us yet."

We repeated these nice bicycle rides every day of that week.

Jordan

Jordan wrote: "Julia, I love you so much! Good night, my love, sleep well!"

Thursday, 19 March 2020
First time Distance Fitness

Distance Fitness was my way of giving something to the people living in my neighbourhood. One of my neighbours had the idea, telling me over the balcony, "You should offer fitness classes for all of us here, every evening. That would be fun, would keep us fit and socially in contact, despite the distance."

This is how 'Distance Fitness' was created and realised, starting on Thursday, 19 March 2020.

I started teaching Distance Fitness for our courtyard, or more precisely, for the people – mostly women – who were living here. They could participate there or on their balconies or in their rooms with the windows open.

Louis

Thanks to this neighbour's idea, this is how, with my music and loudspeaker, I started this enchanting and very successful class. Many women participated on their balconies and with a lot of enthusiasm. Other people came from outside like Tony, Maria, Dina, Winfried and many others, while Louis posted his fitness classes on Facebook!

Tony

Every evening, or nearly every evening, Tony attended the Distance Fitness. He asked me out and with all restaurants and shops closed he asked, "Shall we go for a walk?"

"See you tomorrow for a walk!"

"Well, tomorrow I am already busy, sorry."

"Ok, see you for Distance Fitness!"

Saturday, 21 March 2020

Tony

Tony called and inquired, "How did your meeting with that man from Meetyourlove go?"

"Which one?"

"The one you told me about."

"Ah, yes, ok..."

"You should upload your classes on to YouTube!"

Louis

While teaching his online sports classes, Louis used to say, "Never give up!"

Aky

In the meantime, I had stopped being too pushy with Aky, and as I thought he would, he only replied to messages if I wrote them. From his side, no initiative. Not one single time did he ask if we could meet again or if he could call me. Not once did he even ask if he could do anything for me, if I needed help, or if I was lonely and needed some company. Nothing.

For my part. I simply inquired via WhatsApp: "How are you? Are you ok? Do you want to call?"

His reply: "I am fine. I need to go to buy food but am not hungry enough yet. I am happy to talk later."

As I said before, I can read between the lines. 'I am happy to talk later' means he doesn't want to talk. I waited and this was a test. A real test. Would he call me back?

I remembered the words of Caroline. She had talked about her own experience with dating men from the online dating platforms and said, "When I realised what kind of men where on there, I decided I would find a man somewhere else, anywhere but absolutely not online. They all had a serious problem, mental problems."

Sunday, 22 March 2020

Louis

We all, the entire world it seemed, went online to learn, visiting YouTube, Facebook, Skype, Zoom, Webex, you name them. Louis, as a sports instructor, had started teaching online and taught his second sports fitness class online on Facebook at ten in the morning. This one was a huge success, with nearly a hundred people attending, compared to less than ten the day before. Louis repeatedly said, "Never give up!" during the class. This is my motto too: "Never give up!"

Thursday, 11 June 2020

Nearly three months have gone by. Luxembourg has re-opened, or at least partially, after the complete lockdown. In the first days after 13 March 2020, literally everybody stayed at home. There was nobody on the streets for quite a few weeks. As cyclists, this was a dream situation for Carl and me. We met nearly every day to go riding. In those three months, I cycled over three thousand kilometres on a racing bike, and additionally about three hundred on a mountain bike. For me, this was exceptional, just absolutely outstanding.

From the point of view of biking, this was the best time of my life. Unfortunately, it came to an end with the end of the lockdown. Every day of the lockdown began to look identical. In the early morning, I would teach my online classes. They were via a platform or via video-call. One sports class would also be via video-call, which gave my mother the opportunity to participate as well. Her own class had been cancelled, as it had been in-presence teaching, at the outbreak of the coronavirus crisis.

In the afternoon, Carl and I would meet every day, or nearly every day, for the cycling. The usually dangerous streets – normally overrun with frenetic cars and trucks – were empty, a paradise on earth. Punctually on Friday 13 March 2020, the sun had come out and stayed for the following weeks and months. After a rainy and cold winter, exactly on the day of the lockdown, the sun had come out and stayed. We were happily cycling every day in the sunshine. During the first days of the confinement we used to meet at my place. Carl would come by bike from his home and return by bike. We rode our bikes together starting from my place. In these first days of the lockdown, we mainly cycled around Luxembourg city.

Luxembourg under lockdown

By bike from my place, it is very easy to get to the Pétrusse Valley and the bike path to Hesperange. We always started by following the Pétrusse River and then the Alzette River until we got to Hesperange, with its castle ruins and beautiful park with a lake, flowers and an art exhibition. We used to relax on the grass, looking at the lake with the ducks.

Otherwise, we could begin from my apartment and bike down to the Pétrusse Valley but at Sheffield's Pub, we went uphill to the Wenzel Way and back again downhill to Paffendal and then on to the cycle path to Mersch, Walferdange, Heisdorf, Lorentzweiler, Lintgen and Mersch. In Mersch, it goes uphill and then downhill to Pissingen. Yes, funny name. Pissingen has picturesque castle ruins called Waasserbuerg Pëtten.

If we were looking for some variety, we crossed the city of Luxembourg to go to the path to Senningerberg. Starting again from my apartment, you take the bicycle bridge under the Adolphe Bridge – yes, this is a bicycle and pedestrian bridge UNDER the bridge that was built during the renovations in 2018. Cars drive over it, while everybody else can go under or, depending on how you look at it, through the bridge!

We then went through the parks that encircle the city centre and exited them at the Kinnekswiss Park at the normally extremely busy Robert Schuman roundabout at the Glacis carpark and in front of the Grand Théâtre de la Ville de Luxembourg, with the Pescatore retirement home on the right. We rode over the Red Bridge – officially called Pont Grande-Duchesse Charlotte, although everybody calls it 'Roud Bréck', or the Red Bridge – so named because of its colour, its piers are painted red but the railings are white. Therefore, while you are on it you see it as white but everybody else sees it as red.

We continued on the bike path with the Luxembourg Philharmonic building on the right before passing through the hub of the Kirchberg with its banks, financial institutions, European institutions, the European Court of Justice and the European Investment Bank, until we got to shopping centre and the cinema, ending with the hospital and the exhibition centre – la Foire – and up to the roundabout with the tram station. It was here that we entered the forest, with the bike path following the highway all the way to Trier in Germany.

A little further past the roundabout on the right side is the Luxembourg airport. From here, there are two different paths: one goes east down the hill besides Senningerberg castle to Oberanven and then to Niederanven and Roodt-sur-Syre, while the other goes north through the forest and downhill to Rameldange, Ernster, and following the former railway line, called Charly, to Gonderange. The path here is built on the old rails. This train used to link various villages with the city of Luxembourg, climbing the difficult ascent and the crossing through the forest of Senningerberg.

If we decided to cycle west from my place, we took the bike path to Dippach. This led us through Belair and Merl, suburbs of the city with beautiful gardens and trees blossoming pink and white. After Strassen, we continued through the fields to Mamer where the European school is, or at least the new half of it, the older half being in Kirchberg.

After Mamer, we went through more fields, and forests on the right. There was a farm around here with an amazing huge bull, as well as cows, horses and goats. In springtime these animals had given birth and we loved looking at the little ones. From there, we continued to Garnich. Normally, on the days before the first of May, they hold the 'Elsy Jacobs' a cycling competition over three or four days honouring the Luxembourger who became the first women's Road World Champion. However, in 2020, it was cancelled for coronavirus reasons, along with all other major public events.

From Garnich, we cycled to Kahler and then on to Grass, just at the Belgium border, with its water tower built like a cone. On a previous occasion I had toured the tower with Jordan, when the water services of Luxembourg and the SES water company held an open day. Grass and Kahler are on a hill and from here we had outstanding views to Belgium, the highway to Belgium and the *Zone Industrielle*.

Spring was in the air and every day the temperature rose. We changed from our winter dress to short sleeves and shorts. Flowers came out and we took the best pictures ever.

Because of the lockdown and with no cars on the streets and no planes in the air, the air became unbelievably clear. The sky was clean, a wonderful clean blue. We could see so far, much further than usual. There were no airplanes in the sky, no cars on the streets, no trucks, no building works, no dust and no pollution. Knowing these were unique moments, the beauty of the colours, the special smell of the flowers and the blossoming trees will for ever remain in our memories.

After a while, Carl and I decided to change the routine and meet on our bicycles somewhere on the road between his place and mine. We met at Kockelscheuer, where the most beautiful flowers grew, or at Schléiwenhaff in Leudelange and we rode our bikes happily on these beautiful streets without cars. It was just us, the bikes, the grass or the forest, and the sky.

We joked, "Our Prime Minister Xavier Bettel said 'stay home!' So, we are staying home! We are staying in Luxembourg and visiting all of it!" Among other sites, Carl showed me the statue of the Pissinger Kueben in Pissange! A funny name indeed!

With the confinement continuing, after a while, we went further afield, for longer rides. We met in Frisange and cycled to Mondorf. We enjoyed the recreational park with its magnificent flowers. In Burmerange, Carl showed me the

Maus Ketty – a mouse statue based on a story by Auguste Liesch featuring wine drinking and dancing mice.

We went to the Moselle River, to Remich and to Remerschen, delighting in the wonderfully quiet river with exceptionally clean water and the vineyards in this wine-growing area. We stopped at a small wooden hut at a water-skiing place where we had a break and a picnic.

We cycled between Luxembourg and France. There were small country lanes that wandered into France, although the country was under lockdown without no entry allowed. We cycled through fields and on the heights with views of Cattenom, the nuclear power plant just over the border in France.

Because of the lockdown, in Schengen the road was blocked to both Germany, over the bridge, and to France along the Moselle River. Jean-Claude Juncker expressed his unhappiness about the closure of the borders, as the very meaning of Schengen treaty and Europe is free circulation and open borders. Now, because of the lockdown, all borders in Europe were closed. For Luxembourg, this was an unusual situation, with its hundreds of thousands of daily cross-border commuters now confined to their homes in France, Germany and Belgium.

It was impossible to get into Germany. The border to Germany is the Moselle River with only few bridges that were completely closed, barricaded and manned by the police. It was impossible to go for a ride on the other side of the Moselle. We regretted this very much.

Over the weeks and with the lockdown taking longer, we ended up visiting the entire country.

The only airplanes in the sky were the ones transporting freight. Otherwise there were no planes at all. The sky was of such a never-before-seen blue. All planes were obliged to stay on the ground: an unusual situation, with many job losses foreseen.

In the west of the country, there is another bike path on old train rails. This is from Grass to Clémency and onwards to Bascharage, with the train station there being a bar called Brasserie Op der Gare, where you can normally sit at one of the tables to have a picnic. With the lockdown, the restaurant was closed and the tables were off limits. The former railway lines in the forest went to the border to Belgium, just on the other side of the fence.

One day, we visited the gorgeous castle at Sanem, which was a real surprise for me. The other castles we visited were ruins, but Sanem castle had been rebuilt and beautifully restored and run by the town council. It was stunning and we went inside the courtyard with the gardens in progress. Soon there would be flowers blossoming and birds singing.

Easing of the lockdown

Finally, the lockdown began to be eased with construction works being the first to open again.

The first noticeable change was the increase in traffic on the streets.

People were so edgy; it was obvious that the beautiful times on the quiet and empty streets were over.

On the other hand although it would have been something frivolous and inconsequential before the lockdown, the hairdressers eventually re-opened. With all of them closed, people were not getting a proper haircut and there were strange new trends in hairstyles. For elderly women especially a weekly trip to the hairdressers was a vital social link and now they could go again.

We met one or two more times in Leudelange, where the waffle maker 'Jean La Gaufre' had recently installed his caravan just in front of the church to enjoy a *gaufre* – a waffle– with strawberries, the best strawberry waffle ever. I was so happy.

My happiness cannot be described. I was happy. That's all.

Since the lockdown on 13 March, I had adopted a new rhythm. In the mornings, I would be teaching my online classes until lunch time, and in the afternoon, I would be cycling with Carl, in the beautiful, ever-changing countryside of Luxembourg.

One of the things that really saved us, I think, was the wonderful weather starting from the day of the lockdown. It had been a miserable – and fairly typical – late winter and early spring in Luxembourg. Nature seemed to explode with colours and fragrances every day after this.

We took so many pictures. It is a little unbelievable how many we took.

During the lockdown, nature took back its place from humans and proved itself to be most beautiful. I have never seen such wonderful colours, smelled such lovely scents and seen such views. With the air being pure and clean, the views over the country were outstanding. Unforgettable, this was an unforgettable experience! We saw birds, cows, bulls, horses, rabbits and even some deer.

On one of our last excursions, we climbed up the forest near Soleuvre, all the way up to the ruins of an ancient castle with a huge stone tower – I think its name is St Jean – situated exactly at the top of the hill. Now a ruin that lies in the sun, surrounded by forest.

......

As the lockdown was eased more and more, car traffic increased but in a way that seemed out of proportion, reflecting, I think, the degree of people's nervousness.

For our own security, Carl suggested we should change to mountain biking in the Terre Rouge – Red Rock – area near Dudelange. As I was not a specialist in the sport and I just had bought a new mountain bike, we went to give it a try.

Obviously, I needed some specialised shoes, which Carl bought for me. We continued meeting every day in the Terre Rouge, where he showed me how to ride on the more difficult terrain, and over the days and weeks, I became more confident. The weather remained beautiful, hot, and sunny. Temperatures heated up even more over the next few weeks, reaching thirty degrees and above.

We cycled the Ellergronn and Haard areas, mainly the Haard, Hesselsbierg and Staebierg. The soil there, as well as the stones and the rocks, is red, which is a pleasing contrast to the green trees. Luxembourg's wealth was built up from the mid-nineteenth century from the mining industry. The banking, financial and services sectors came later. We visited the entrances of the mines and saw that there were many holes in the ground from collapsed underground galleries. We took pictures of old coal and steam trains, the railway station, the national mining museum, the funicular and the wagons, delighting in the most amazing views over the valley from the top of the rocks.

In Fonds-de-Gras and La Sauvage we visited the forest and the old mines while cycling and hiking.

In Belval, at the main campus of the University of Luxembourg there is still a blast furnace from top of which there are excellent views of the area, which was formerly heavily industrialised with iron and steel production. It is now a university and residential district with shops, a cinema and an ambitious project to integrate the past and the future.

In Dudelange there is a district called 'Little Italy' with a *Boulodrome* where Italians used to – and still do – play pétanque. On the other side of the railway is the Documentation Centre for Human Migrations. Many Italian migrants used to work in the Luxembourg steel industry and there is a statue representing the migrants arriving in the country. It was Carl's idea to show me all of this in detail and, my interest awoken, I looked everything up on the internet and discovered that it was known as the Minett tour.

One day, we rode up to the Léiffrächen monument erected for the people who worked in the mines. This is a high tower that can be seen from afar and the view from the top is stunning. Over one thousand four hundred names of mine workers who lost their lives in the mines are inscribed on the stone plaques that make up the monument.

During our mountain bike tours, we sat on benches and looked over the countryside, having views of Tétange, Rumelange and Kayl. We took photos everywhere we went. People would be relaxing on the grass, having picnics and enjoying the sun. We would sit on the grass at a spot that overlooked the old mining sites, with the new University of Luxembourg in the foreground.

This part of the Red Rock area is close to the French border; in fact we often cycled parallel with the fence or the border markers. Had it not been for the coronavirus crisis, we could have crossed the border and visited the old mining zones of Volmerange-les-Mines, Kanfen and Ottange in France.

Unlike the forest, the streets had become so dangerous because of increased traffic that it was risking one's life while riding the bikes on the streets. Actually, several cyclists were injured by car drivers and unfortunately there were also cyclists who were killed after collisions with delivery vans.

The beautiful times were over.

Beginning and mid-May

From the beginning of May to the end of the month, we celebrated several birthdays. These were held outside in the courtyard, with social distancing and our masks of course.

I divided my cycling and hiking time between Carl, Alan and Jordan and Jasmine.

It was a beautiful time.

Alan and I stayed in touch by phone, we called or texted every day. When I was free, I went cycling with him. We talked about my online teaching, writing, his job, the newspapers he was reading, politics, the coronavirus and about the impact the crisis would have on the world economy and on people's mental health.

Alan said, "This is a revolution. Nothing will remain unchanged after this period. People will not want to return to the office. They will want to work remotely, from home or from wherever they are."

For many people this meant job losses, sadness and, most frightening of all, the loss of loved ones. It was the time of coronavirus and people were getting sick, then hospitalised and then died in hospital. We were watching the news every day. Terrible reports came from Italy and Spain, where so many people died. Many companies closed. Restaurants and shops remained shut for about three months. This was a financial disaster. Airlines suffered greatly because of the travel ban. No flights, absolutely no flights. The airplanes stayed on the ground at the airports and many employees would lose their jobs.

Car factories did not produce cars and did not sell the cars they had produced. Where to put all these unsold cars?

Shops were closed for three months and people bought everything online. Online shopping volumes jumped massively. That's why there was an increase in freight flights in Luxembourg: to deliver all those Amazon parcels – and, of course, the masks.

Use of online video conferencing with Skype, Zoom, Webex or WhatsApp calls increased exponentially. They could all be used for free.

Elderly people, being in the high-risk category, were asked not to meet in person but to chat through a video conference.

Saarbrücken

Alan and I went to Saarbrücken, to go cycling along the Saar River. We started in Saarbrücken city centre, stayed on the Fahrradweg – the cycle path – and crossed into France and then continued straight until Sarreguemines.

The people we met on the bike path were mostly very aggressive, uneasy and unfriendly. We decided to stop, get off our bikes and talk with some people to get an understanding of what was going on. People said they were afraid, anxious because of the lockdown and of the enormous economic impact. Some had lost money or jobs, some had lost both. They felt isolated and were uncertain what the future would bring. They hated uncertainty. Also, being confined with the same person or people in a small apartment or house is challenging. They all said they were tired of being locked down. The kids were difficult and it was hard to do work at the same time that they were playing, or their partner had other things to do. Instead of being out with colleagues and friends, always being at home with the same faces was an issue.

On 28 May, *bars, pubs and restaurants were allowed to progressively re-open, starting with spaces outside and the following week inside areas could be opened, although masks were required.*

Slowly, people and life returned to Luxembourg city centre.

Shops re-opened on 3 June 2020. It was possible to go shopping in a real shop, not online shopping. Can you imagine!? I went shopping for the first time after lockdown. It was a strange experience after such a long time.

Pentecost

From Pentecost onwards, Distance Fitness was once a week; Friday evenings at a quarter to seven as I had reduced the frequency. Before Pentecost, I had taught Distance Fitness every evening starting with Tony, Maria, Dina, Winfried, Jordan, Jasmine and many others attending. I didn't miss one single day. Sometimes though, I arrived late, because I returned from mountain biking in Terre Rouge, spending the afternoon with Carl. I greatly enjoyed that time with him, finishing the afternoon sitting at a picnic table with Carl and I talking about this astonishing mining area, while he told me everything about the rich history that I often would look up later on the internet.

We had decided that Distance Fitness would last all summer. We had our regulars in place and my colleague Eleni came to do Zumba with us. This was most enjoyable as it was a change from my general fitness classes of before.

Saarburg

On Tuesday, 2 June, Carl and I cycled to Saarburg. This was such a wonderful day! We had had amazing days, but this was one of the highlights. We drove from my place to Grevenmacher and parked just over the bridge on the German side in a car park. Along the German side, we followed the bike path to the *Saarmündung*, where the Saar River flows into the Moselle River and, instead of taking the bridge to Trier, we went under the bridge to Saarburg. We sat on a bench and enjoyed the view of Saarburg castle, which we later climbed up to and from where we had amazing views of the vineyards, the Saar River, and Saarburg town. We also went to eat an ice cream, the tradition here, and to sit next to the river with the famous waterfall. There we sat and enjoyed the heat – over thirty degrees – before heading back.

These were happy days.

During the first week of June, Carl and I met every single day of the week and spent so much time together. It really was the best time of my life.

Terre Rouge - Red Rock

On Saturday, 6 June, Carl and I had been mountain biking in Terre Rouge, as we had many times before, and we were sitting on a bench when he said to me, "Why do all women get mad at me when they don't get what they want?" I took this remark badly. Just before this he had asked me if I were interested in going on a holiday with him to a place where there is no Wi-Fi, and I had said, "I need Wi-Fi. You know that I need Wi-Fi."

"But I don't need Wi-Fi," he replied.

I said, "That is narcissistic."

"What has that got to do with narcissism?" he asked.

We remained silent for a long while. I felt his inner anger, his aggression.

On Sunday, 7 June, Carl invited me for lunch at our favourite restaurant. He had been mountain biking with his friends in the morning at La Rochette, with its medieval castle ruins. They had planned to be cycling all day, but his friends didn't feel well and so they cut their bike ride short. Carl called me to ask me out for lunch. He didn't want to go home to his children. In the restaurant, with social distancing of course, the tables were spaced out. The table was disinfected, a paper tablecloth was laid out, the menu was replaced by a phone app and the waitress had her mask, although she hadn't lost her beauty and her friendliness. We talked. It was such a pleasure having a chat with someone in a restaurant after such a long time while enjoying good food. It was just a usual Sunday, one would have said before the coronavirus crisis. Now, it was special.

In June 2020

Carl

One day at the beginning of June, Carl was in an extremely bad mood. "What's up?" I asked. "Nothing," he replied. I tried again a bit later and asked, "Is there anything not ok?" He repeated, "Nothing." He had come by car, despite the fact that we had said we would go cycling from my apartment into town, as it was raining in Terre Rouge but the sun was out in the city. I asked him again when we went out for a walk, "So, tell me, what's on your mind?" His reply was always the same: "Nothing." I also asked, "Do you want to drink something?" His reply: "No." I asked again, "Really not?" He snapped back, "Why can't women accept when I say no." He was irritable. After our walk in the Pétrusse Valley, we returned to his car and just before leaving he said, "It's better if I stay at home for the next few days." He drove off angrily.

I did not hear from him anymore. He did not write or phone. I waited for him to write one day. Or phone.

By this time, the lockdown was definitely coming to an end. The local airline had started flying again to selected destinations. Our best time was over.

Alan

This is when Alan asked me to go cycling with him.

"Julia, do you want to come for a ride with me?"

"Yes, shall we meet on the Hesperange cycle path and go from there?"

When we met, Alan said, "You have to watch the YouTube link I sent you. Fantozzi, he is a genius!"

We talked about Fantozzi and his 1972 film called 'After the Quarantine'. How could he have come up with such a film in 1972? It all seemed to be so prophetic now in 2020 – just incredible and astounding.

Alan later said, "Julia, you are so beautiful! You are so good looking! You have never changed, after all of these years! You are still the same, smiling, dream woman! You are my dream woman, the woman I always dreamt of! You represent all I want a woman to be!"

Jordan

In the evening, Jordan sent me a text message: "Julia, I love you! Let's meet for a bike ride tomorrow. Or can we go for a walk? Or maybe you want to go to the drive-in cinema with me? I have never been to one, please come with me! We could do both: in the afternoon a walk in the forest, or bicycle and in the evening the drive-in!"

Tony

Tony phoned and asked, "Is there any Distance Fitness tonight?"

"Yes, I said there would be!"

"Ok, I am coming!"

LOVE AND CORONAVIRUS

Love in coronavirus times!

What do you think about when you think of coronavirus times?

On the TV, on the radio or talking with friends, there are always the same questions everywhere.

I look at the sky. There are swallows flying in the blueness, a few white clouds in the distance and the sun is beginning to set: it is late evening. Approaching 21 June, these are the longest days of the year. After that, we will lose daylight again. I am feeling sentimental and sitting alone on my balcony, which I call lovingly 'my office' – the best office in the world.

I am sad, because I am alone again. It was just a dream. Indeed, Carl will never be mine, even though we spent the most extraordinary times together. I am sad. Tears run down my cheeks.

Trier

The next day, I thought, this is not right. This is not good. I wrote, phoned and left messages for Carl telling him how much I love him. I cried my eyes out. Late in the evening, he replied, finally. We would meet for a bike ride on Saturday afternoon and take the cycle path to Trier, with its Porta Nigra, its cathedral and its lively pedestrian zone, where one can eat a fruit cake and drink a coffee while watching people. Because of the coronavirus, we would have to wear our masks.

On Saturday, 13 June 2020, exactly three months to the day since the start of lockdown, Carl and I went to Trier.

I asked him, "Carl, why didn't you write or phone?"

"You didn't write or phone either!" Carl said, with a smile, "I was waiting for you to contact me first."

"Never do this to me again, you had me worried!"

"A little break is good from time to time!" he replied smiling, and then he kissed me, "I love you!"

Since the beginning of March this year, all public transport is free in Luxembourg, which is extremely convenient, despite the ongoing coronavirus pandemic. So, with our masks on our faces, we took the train to Wasserbillig. Our bikes were in the bike compartment and we enjoyed the views from the windows. When we got to Wasserbillig, we rode to the ferry pier, where the small ferry boat took us to the other side of the Moselle River to Oberbillig in Germany. Exactly when we got on the ferry, it started raining lightly, but this was not a bother for us on the bike path to Trier, which is not too far and without uphill or downhill stretches either, just straight and flat into Trier. When we got there, we saw that the city centre was packed with shoppers. After such a long lockdown, this was a blessing for the shop owners. We took in all the tourist sights and rode back to the ferry. There was no rain now as we headed back to the Luxembourgish side of the Moselle River.

"There should be a train leaving from the station every half an hour back to Luxembourg," said Carl. We arrived at the station just to see the train leave, which was funny.

"Shall we have a Kebab while waiting for the next one?" I suggested, "There is a Kebab shop just down the road."

"Yes, very good idea!" We went there to eat our Durum on the terrace outside and chatted and laughed. I said, "Shall we go now to catch the next train?"

"Ok!"

We arrived at the station, just to see, for the second time, the train leaving for Luxembourg right in front of our noses!

Carl laughed and said, "That is hilarious! Twice missing the train by a few seconds! Now we will stay here and wait for the next one! It leaves from platform two. This is the slow train, it will stop at each and every village and will take nearly as long as the fast train, leaving half an hour later, but never mind! This is really funny!"

After more than forty-five minutes, we arrived in Luxembourg city.

Alan

Alan wrote this message: "I am now at a bike event in the north of Luxembourg. We will ride seven hundred kilometres this week, all within Luxembourg. Initially we wanted to cycle from Luxembourg through Belgium and then to the Netherlands, but unfortunately because of the coronavirus restrictions, our event couldn't be done in a normal way, as it would have included transportation in mini-buses, accommodation in hotels and cycling in a group on the streets. Therefore, we decided to remain in Luxembourg in one hotel from which we will depart every morning and return to every evening. The days are long and the weather will be fine. We are sure to be able to do our week's trip here. Hope you are fine. It is not easy for you, as an independent worker, some days you are ok, other days you are down. Please don't worry. Everything will be all right."

Monday, 15 June 2020

Thomas

Thomas tried to contact me again after all these weeks of coronavirus lockdown. He sent various text messages that I didn't reply to.

Carl

Besides riding our racing bikes and mountain biking, we also went climbing, Carl and I. After the coronavirus lockdown, a local climbing wall opened up again this Monday, after a three-month shutdown. It's hard to believe that three months had already gone by since we last went climbing together. A friend of ours came with us for the climbing. "I have forgotten everything," I said.

The wall was in Dudelange inside a sports centre. A limited number of climbers were allowed into the hall. The afternoon at the wall went well, without any incidents and everybody climbed happily.

Thursday, 18 June 2020

After a short period of rain, there was sunshine again. The sun was out and it was warm – a very comfortable twenty-six degrees. We met in Mondorf-les-Bains at the car park of the spa. As it was summer there were fewer flowers in the parks. We were on our racing bikes and rode through a park and then to Burmerange, to see the *Maus Ketty* statue. There were views from the hill over the south of Luxembourg and into France, including the nuclear power plant in Cattenom. "If one day there is an accident here like in Chernobyl, we all are dead," I remarked. We continued downhill to Schengen castle in the 'three-country corner' covering Luxembourg, France and Germany. There was a lovely cherry tree just in front of the castle with ripe cherries which we ate. The European Schengen Area covers more than four million square kilometres and enfolds a population of around four hundred and twenty million people. Schengen town, from where the treaty gets its name, or rather it is probably more accurate to say Schengen village, has an area of just thirty-one square kilometres and a population of under five thousand. Besides the treaty signed there, it is known for its vineyards and its location on the Moselle River in Luxembourg, bordering Germany and France. We crossed the bridge to Germany and took the cycle path along the Moselle, to Remich, also known for its vineyards and a bridge over the river. The path that follows the Moselle to Koblenz is three hundred and sixty-four kilometres long!

"I have an idea!" I said, "We could go by train to Bernkastel-Kues and Traben-Trarbach and ride from there and return in the evening. The days are long, we could do this, isn't that a great idea? You know I don't like to cycle with bags and so we wouldn't need to sleep over night in a hotel."

"That's a very good idea! Let's see when we could do this."

Jordan

"Julia, what about going to the drive-in? I have never been to a drive-in, watching a movie in your car sounds fun to me! Please come with me!"

"Why don't you go there with Jasmine?"

"Oh yeah, that's an excellent idea!"

"We could go cycling, the three of us, to Munsbach castle, with the flower garden, if you wish, next Sunday afternoon. What do you think?"

"Great, we'll do that! On Saturday evening we are having a dinner in my garden, although because of coronavirus, we'll need to keep our distance. But the good news is now I am cooking! I have never cooked before in my life but, now, because of coronavirus I am experimenting with loads of different recipes."

Jasmine noted with a smile, "Luckily we have this coronavirus crisis, this was the only way to get you cooking."

No internet access

With coronavirus restrictions eased and borders re-opened, we continued our cycling afternoons. We went often around town or on the bike path to Hesperange and back. One day, I cycled from Luxembourg to Hesperange and back three times. This was on a rather difficult day when I didn't have any Internet.

In the morning, I had been working normally on my computer, using Wi-Fi as usual, when suddenly the connection cut out. I called the provider, but there was no reply. I took my 'Fritz-Box' to the provider's office but the employee there told me that it was working perfectly.

I went back home again and checked: still no Internet. After a few attempts to call the provider's office repair people without reply I gave up and went to another office. The young lady told me that I had to call them. I tried to tell her this is exactly what I had been trying to do all morning. She insisted. "Ok, I'll go back home and call again," I said. And finally, I succeeded in getting through and explained my issue. The man on the phone told me "There is no connection to your home, we will check and try to fix it."

I was desperate. Internet is essential for me and it was an emotional shock. I went to my neighbour on the third floor. "I have no Internet. But I need to work," I told him, "Do you have Internet?" He replied, "Yes, I do. I can give you access to my Wi-Fi. Here is the login code." This was really kind of him. I went back to my apartment and logged in with his credentials; he has another provider. And it worked. Luckily. What would we do without the Internet? I felt quite shocked.

I worked on what I had to do, teach via Skype, grade my students, write emails and so on. I went for a ride to forget about this frightening experience. Three times from Luxembourg to Hesperange and back. I met Carl in Hesperange park and we rode together. "How are you?" he asked. "I was fine until twenty past nine this morning," I said, "when my Wi-Fi connection broke down and I didn't have Wi-Fi anymore. Luckily my neighbour gave me access through his. We really depend on Wi-Fi, especially in coronavirus times."

The next day, Saturday afternoon, my Wi-Fi returned. Later, I learned from other neighbours that this had been a general problem with that provider. All their lines had been busy because everybody was calling and some banks were also affected. "Maybe with the street works all over, some street worker cut the main fibre cable," I suggested to my neighbours over the balcony. "Maybe, who knows," they replied, "What we know is that there were many people concerned about having this provider. The other companies had no issues that day."

Carl later said, "It is important to have different accesses to the internet from different providers, just to avoid such emergency situations. As you depend so much on the internet, you need to have a back-up solution in case one Wi-Fi fails."

I thought about all those people who, during the lockdown, had not had such a lifeline. Some people were not so lucky as us and internet access was difficult for them.

Saturday, 4 July 2020: Independence Day

Carl

On this same Saturday afternoon in July, which was the 4th of July to be exact, we wanted to take the train to Trier and cycle along the Moselle River. I met Carl at the train station as he had come by train from his place. But then we saw what I had already understood from the Internet: there were no trains to Trier today and tomorrow, because of works.

"Very well," I said, "let's ride from here then, instead of losing all this time on public transport."

"Where do you want to go to?"

"North-east. Let's head to Echternach on the bike path!"

This particular path is the former railroad to Echternach. It was converted into a cycle path that runs through a lovely forest. There is also a well-known train tunnel near Bech, which, it turned out, is refreshing in summer because the temperature inside is low while outside it is hot. In winter, it is cold and humid in the tunnel.

In Consdorf, we visited a monument that was made up of a bomb that had been uncovered there after the Second World War. There were three flags flying: Luxembourgish, European and American. The wind only blew the first two while the stars and stripes were hanging low.

I said, "It is Independence Day today but with the current events in the USA not even the flag wants to blow in the wind."

He said, "With fifty-five thousand new coronavirus infections every day, the USA holds a sad record these days. Not to mention the fact that this Independence Day people are partying, drinking and enjoying themselves at beaches and everywhere else, without masks or social distancing, and at the fireworks in Washington for President Donald Trump, many more new infections will happen today. While we cycle alone in the forest, they don't keep their social distancing requirements."

"Do you see these cherries up there in the tree?" I exclaimed, "They are so ripe, they are black, not red. Let's try them, they must be exceptionally tasty!" And they really were tasty; as tasty as the cherries we had eaten from the tree in Remich, at the Moselle, but with a different taste. When cherries are warm from the sun and picked directly from the tree and popped into the mouth, they are delicious! Carl said, "If you take them home, tomorrow, they will not taste the same. There is nothing more delicious than sun-warmed cherries eaten from the tree."

Jordan

The same week, I did almost the same ride with Jordan, going to Senningerberg from Kirchberg, to Hostert, Charly's Gare, down to Niederanven and Mensdorf until Munsbach and to the castle, where exquisite roses were flowering in front of the restored castle. In the July sun the roses smelt sweet. There were not only roses, but all kinds of other flowers, all named with little plaques in front of them. Numerous bees were flying between them and landing on the flowers.

On another occasion during the same week, Jordan and I cycled again from Kirchberg to Hostert, but then continued on the bike path heading to Echternach. At Ernster, we took the 'Syre' path and admired the fine-looking houses built there with breath-taking views to the west and east, all the way to Germany. On our way back, we encountered a group of cyclists that included Carl. They were so fast and they flew by in a millisecond without even noticing us.

"I want you to be part of my family," Jordan said, "I want to share my children with you! I want to marry you!"

Alan

Also during this time, Alan and I were still keeping on being friends, phoning, messaging, meeting, going cycling together or meeting by chance in the Pétrusse Valley. His current girlfriend was living far away and, because of coronavirus travel restrictions, he hadn't been able to fly to see her, and even if he could there would be two weeks quarantine. When these were lifted, he went by car to see her. It was a long drive.

Since mid-June, Distance Fitness had been twice a week – every Tuesday and Friday evening – because people had asked to have it two times a week instead of only one. Regulars included Eleni, Tony, Maria, Dina, Winfried, Jordan, Jasmine and Carmen. We had now included Zumba and Pilates, stretching, general fitness and all kinds of other sports. Gratifyingly, they had even asked me if we could continue the Distance Fitness not only over summer but also after summer.

SOME WISE REFLECTIONS

Some final words, written on 14 July 2020

This book is the story about my dating experiences during the coronavirus pandemic.

My story started sometime in March 2019 and stops today as I write these sentences. It tells of my dating experiences with different men, all of them treasured and appreciated, and the ongoing worldwide Covid-19 crisis. How it continues, only the future will tell us!

In the times of coronavirus, I joined the online platform Meetyourlove.org to combat my loneliness because my long-time boyfriend had left me. Since then, I have met many diverse men. The different meetings make up this book.

On Friday, 13 March 2020, the entire country was locked down because of Covid-19.

From the beginning of July 2020, the lockdown measures were slowly lifted step by step in Luxembourg and elsewhere around the world with mixed results. Some cities and countries had to close down again because of rising numbers of cases. Other cities even talked about having no face masks. Some flights restarted, only to some destinations but not to all. People started flying for holidays while others took their cars. Borders were opened inside Europe and also partially outside Europe. These were uncertain times. Some people were wearing face masks, others were not. Some people kept to social distancing, others did not. This resulted in rises in coronavirus cases in Luxembourg and worldwide.

Will there be a second wave of coronavirus? A second complete shutdown? Will a vaccine be discovered soon? Will the entire world be vaccinated? What will happen next? How many people will suffer? Die? Will there be another, different virus? When? What?

Many questions arise. There are still many subjects for discussion on our bikes.

However complex my inner emotions and feelings are, putting them on paper helped me overcome my sorrow, while describing even more complex personal relationships and places of interest in Luxembourg, with its beautiful countryside and rich history. What held me especially were the colours, smells and fragrances of the plants: tulips, roses, lime trees, apple trees, cherry trees, and the corn, wheat, rye and oat fields. They all smelt differently, with different colours, ranging from yellow, to pink, red, blue and the deep red-black of the ripe cherries on the tree in Remich. I also recall fondly the pink in the blossoming of the cherry trees in Mondorf-les-Bains and the yellow in the rapeseed fields in Garnich. My inner feelings are sometimes so deep, ranging the full bandwidth from thoughtfulness to despair, from anger through to irritation and to more positive emotions like hope, friendship and the desire for love.

Many people belittle online dating platforms, even while possibly using them themselves. Despite the criticism, I discovered them to be a wonderful means of fighting negative thoughts, to get away from feelings of loneliness by simply keeping me busy. Busy, busy, busy. Instead of sad, depressed, and lonely.

What kept me going was simply keeping busy while sharing my experiences with different men every day and telling my friends how my various dates with the men went. These men have their emotions, feelings, love, doubts and hesitations, while meeting me, an unknown woman. While sitting on my side of the table facing them, I often tried to imagine being on their side of the table, thinking to myself at the same time "What does he think about me?" "How does he find me?" "What impression do I have on him?" Most of the time, the answer to these questions was the same: "This man thinks I am completely crazy! Completely out of my mind!" With a tear in one eye and a smile in the other, I must say that I think they really looked at me like that.

The men I encountered have their flaws and their virtues, just as I have disadvantages and good qualities for them. It is impossible for me to wholly criticise any one of them. On the other hand, neither can I praise any of them to the skies. As I said, putting myself in their place was the best exercise, seeing me in their eyes made me understand myself better: "What am I looking for, what am I not looking for?" "What kind of relationship am I looking for, what not?"

With the coronavirus lockdown, there was a lot of time for reflection – on change, self-improvement and priorities. "This crisis is an opportunity," was my first thought every morning when opening my eyes. An opportunity for what? This is to be seen!

While checking my WhatsApp contacts, I see Oliver has put up a new profile picture, showing him with a woman next to him. This means he is showing the entire world that he has found his love. Honestly, I am happy for him. He had said to me, "I don't want to be with you, I want to be with someone else." At least he was honest, and at least, in the end, it is a happy end for him. He has found love. He was on a dating platform to find love. If he found his love there or somewhere else, it doesn't matter. What matters is that he found love. He was looking for love and he used the platform to find it. Who cares where he found it? I will never know. Or shall I take to WhatsApp and ask him? Anyway, the dating site helped him to see what he was NOT looking for: me! He was looking for somebody else.

My friend Caroline – she who had received the 'Va te faire foutre sale pute' comment – went through different experiences to finally find a suitable partner outside of the platform.

One Sunday afternoon, on my bike with Carl I saw Aky walking with other people, maybe friends or family. I couldn't stop, I was too fast.

On another occasion, Carl and I met Christophe, all three of us on our bikes, and we all said hello. We all understood the situation.

Jordan sent me this message: "They discovered coronavirus in wastewater and in some places even in drinking water, and people have to boil the drinking water for 10 minutes to make it drinkable. Or is this fake news, Julia, what do you think?"

A brief but enlightening exchange with him followed.

"Shall we go for a bike ride on Sunday?" I asked him.

He replied, "On Sunday, Jasmine and I are going hiking!"

One day, Thomas messaged me again, sending his photos, and from the message I understood he was still searching. One day, he will find the right person, I am sure.

As for me, from my heart, I wish these men good luck with their search. I did not find love on the dating platform either. However, the platform helped me in my search for love, to keep busy, to forget about my loneliness, my sadness, my despair and to finally find the right person, the person I love. To find love and to be no longer alone is an exceptional thing. Loneliness really kills you. Some people I talked to told me that they prefer being on these dating platforms just to be less lonely, even though the encounters with potential partners are not as positive as expected. Still, this is better than being lonely. For me, honestly, I thank my friend who suggested I register on Meetyourlove, against all odds. She helped me in my fight against loneliness, to find love again, to find the right person, the man I love.

Since the day of the lockdown on Friday, 13 March 2020 until today, four months later on 14 July, I have cycled more than three thousand five hundred kilometres in Luxembourg. With many more to come!

The ideas behind my actions: How to find love in times of coronavirus

The basic ideas for my actions here are inspired mainly by two books: first *El amor en los tiempos del cólera - Love in the Time of Cholera* by Gabriel García Márquez; and second *The Start-up of You* by Reid Hoffman and Ben Casnocha.

Love in the Time of Cholera tells of a fifty-year wait to win back a long-lost love. The hero has not been chaste all those years of course, but in the end, he is truthful to himself. It also speaks directly to me about finding new life in difficult times.

On the other hand, *The Start-up of You* is full of good advice and here are some pearls of wisdom from Hoffman and Casnocha[1]:

"Whenever you feel alone:

- *Invest in yourself!*

- *Invest in your network!*

- *Invest in society! Give back to society. Allocate time and money to directly help the community in which you live.*

From the bottom of my heart I recommend their book to everybody who wants to find love, who wants to enjoy life

---

[1] (2013, pp. 224, 225): The Start-up of You. Random House Business Book 2013.

or who wants to have a career. Their advice was the foundation of my actions in this book.

Try to change the world. Do something that is in line with your values and aspirations and make use of your competitive advantages.

The way to achieve differentiation is by NOT doing what everyone else is doing."

Epilogue: What are my dreams?

How did I find love in times of coronavirus?

"What do you think about when you think about coronavirus?" asks the speaker on CNN.

I have a big smile on my face. I think about how I found love in times of coronavirus!

I think about all the unbelievable moments I lived, may I say, the greatest moments of my life. They come to my mind in white clouds on a light sky-blue background:

- Love: looking for love – finding love – living love.

- Unique dating experiences.

- Friendships and relationships.

- Nature! Fantastic nature during complete lockdown, with flowers of all colours, yellow, red, blue, white, green, rose, violet, so bright and shining. The sky was a never-before-seen blue, with such white clouds. There were birds singing in the trees, which were beautifully light green at first then darker green with every day. Then there were the smells, scents of all kinds, clean rivers with fish, sounds of birds singing, animals taking back their space, nature taking back its space from human encroachment.

- Silence.

- Forests, fields and grass.

- Views.

- Bicycling and fitness.

- Free time for living.

- Writing books.

- Online teaching.

- The coronavirus pandemic accelerated digitalisation in general and online education in particular.

The final word: The outlook for the future

Holding hands after a nice bike ride on a warm sunny day, we kiss. He says, "It would be nice, if we could stop time; if we could always be in love the way we are right now!"